LUCY KILLGREW

Murphy Gordon

Copyright © 2007 by Murphy Gordon
Sawmill Publishing
6444 E. Spring Street Suite 215
Long Beach, California 90815
Orders: www.sawmillpublishing.com

Cover art and chapter illustrations by Diane Lucas

Printed in the United States of America

ISBN 978-0-9749915-6-6 PAPERBACK
ISBN 978-0-9749915-7-3 HARDCOVER

To the memory of my mother
Rose

With special thanks to

Billy Two Rivers and the
Mohawk of Kahnawá:ke
for their hospitality

My Amen
Used with permission
Written by Ruth Daniel Hunter
Richmond, Virginia

Foreword

My Amen

You who haunt my house, disturb my dreams,
　　tug at my soul,
I sense you beside me in my mirror, reflecting,
　　reflecting....
Ghostly figures in gray and sunlit silver.
You beckon me and bid my soul to give you credence,
My heart is filled and swells with your persistence.
What of these shadows that make me and all of mine
What we are, cradling our past and shaping
　　our future?
Is my daughter's shining face the legacy of
　　the English woman
Smiling back at me? Is there a Celtic lilt in her
　　childish voice,
Rejoicing, glorifying, imitating, inspiring her to dance
The music of harpists, flutists, that only her soul
Can hear and only her spirit can understand,
　　embracing that
Wild song from afar? Is my son's love of
　　this fragile earth

The gift of those of you who roamed our
    Virginia woodlands,
Or his canoe trip down the James as exciting as that
    of the young sun-bronzed brave I see now and
    then...?
Is our love of freedom born of stuff from twelve
    generations ago
When a score of Dutchmen waved goodbye to friend
    and family
For adventure or death, bestowing on us the
    legacy of discovery?
I hear your footsteps on the march of the Revolution,
    your drums
Beating in unison for valor and honor. I hear the
    dull clank of the
Loosening of chains of slavery. I hear your
    joyous laughter
And eagerly skip to your lively tune....
    skipping, skipping.
I will not suppress you, my Ghosts of the Past.
You rise with me in the morning, kneel beside
    my bed in
Evening prayer and guide this pen as I write.
You tantalize me with glimpses of another time
    and with your promises
Of wondrous tomorrows! Hold my hand,
    give me your vision
And walk with me into those tomorrows. Amen

                           Ruth Daniel Hunter

LUCY KILLGREW

The Nations

IT IS SAID THE rivers tell us many things. They speak to us in languages that are soothing to our hearts and minds. Carrying tiny rocks and stones as they cascade through the rich forests, depositing them at their whim, where they remain to tell stories of distant times and places. Those who come to the river with an open heart and mind may hear of days and dreams gone by. They may even find themselves in the voices of the moving streams as they brush by the life stones of history.

Just after the first Crusade, almost 400 hundred years before Cortez defeated the Aztecs, and centuries before Columbus' arrival in the Americas, the Iroquois were constructing their villages and raising their crops in a world of abundant wildlife and bountiful forests. As the native population increased, so did warfare among the many tribes. Villages grew larger and more fortified as each tribe expanded, encroaching on the territory of other tribes. Consequently, relationships between the various tribes became more strained, resulting in constant war, bloody feuds, and revenge attacks.

Across the ocean, Europe's royalty exercised their might over their own people and neighboring countries with numerous wars accentuated by plague and abject poverty. As the centuries passed, the old world looked upon the new world with increasingly envious eyes.

Before too long, the dominant powers of the known world set their interests on conquering this strange and wonderful place called America. The diseases they brought with them devastated the native populations. They also brought with them new reasons for war and new tools to fight those wars.

In 1702, the Mohawk leader, Theyanoguin, went to Montreal to negotiate an agreement of neutrality. With great effort, the Mohawk, Oneida, Cayuga, Seneca and Onondaga reached an agreement to live in peace with the English and French and, more importantly, themselves. Several years later, the Iroquois League grew to six nations with the inclusion of the Tuscarora tribe.

With this peace came political unity and a military power enabling them to claim vast swaths of territory as their own. They lived in abundance in a communal, matriarchal society and continued to thrive in the land that sustained them.

A little more than fifty years later, the French held Canada in the north and the British held the colonies in the south. Again, calm reigned until the French, under the command of a young French aristocrat named Joseph Coulon de Villiers, Lord of Jumonville, ventured down into the region known as the Forks of the Ohio, encroaching on British territory.

At just about the same time, Virginia Governor Dinwittie dispatched a twenty-two year-old officer by the name of George Washington as a surveyor to oversee the building of a military roadway in the region. The two men, Washington and Coulon de Villiers, met near an area called the Great Meadow on July 3, 1754, and engaged in a skirmish; this skirmish was the beginning of a fight for supremacy that would become known as the French and Indian War. Allied with the French were the Algonquin, Huron, Ojibwa, Ottawa and Shawnee. On the side of the British were the Iroquois. In a fierce struggle that began in 1754 and lasted until the Treaty of Paris in 1763, the French were ultimately defeated and Canada became a part of the British Empire.

King George III now ruled North America. From Canada in the north to the colonies in the south, England was master. Almost as soon as peace settled in, the rattling of sabers, the sparking of flints, and the discharge of muskets had replaced negotiations with the king for basic freedoms. New thoughts; new ideas; a new world. Freedom, like a newborn colt, was stretching its legs. The colonies were in turmoil and families were at odds with one another. The land was teeming with activity and unrest.

This was a time of divided loyalties – loyalty to a king and loyalty to the right to live under a self-governing society. It was a time to choose. These ideals, so inconsequential in the world's timeline, but so significant in the eyes of those of the day, ruled the thoughts and actions of many great men and women. The revolution was just beginning, but deep in the hearts of the colonists, there was still hope that the king could be swayed to come to his senses. But it was not to be. War, again drawing together the alliances of the native tribes - some supporting the colonists and others supporting the British would once again consume the lives of many.

Fate took a hand in the lives of a few ordinary men and women, lifting them above others. Their sacrifices, courage, and honor may have gone unnoticed or even forgotten by the majority of us, but they would carve the path to the future for hundreds of years to come. When this war was over, the world would never be the same.

As the rapidly flowing stream of clear water continued on its journey, a beautiful blue-green stone came to a halt along the riverbank of a Mohawk village.

Chapter One

Flight

Hudson Valley, NY, September 1775

THE MAJESTIC BIRD CIRCLED high above the Mohawk. *Brother Hawk,* thought the Indian, *what things you must feel and see.* As he had seen this wonderful creature before, it seemed to Young John that the hawk and he were on the same path. This was the hawk's home and Young John's trap line crossed into his forest.

I am free, thought Brother Hawk as he danced majestically through the darkening sky. The clean air over the rich forest below him filled his lungs. Stretching his wings wide and riding effortlessly on a rising current of air, the great bird gently tipped his tail slightly to the right, circling the

British patrol gathered in a clearing below.

In the distance, a rumble of thunder momentarily broke the hawk's attention. As droplets of rain bounced off his wings, he knew that it was time to get to a safe place. This was his home. The land stretched as far as his eyes could see and beyond. Fair, tree-brushed hills rolled off into a lush expanse of freshly harvested farmland, the dark, earthen layers pelted by the steady rain. The purplish hues of the twilight began to grow ever grayer as dark, bull-headed clouds billowed in.

Brother Hawk circled lower, searching for a proper place to rest. As the current he had been riding shifted violently, the great bird ducked his head against the wind, taking notice for the first time of the red-clad men heading north through the clearing. The men appeared as indiscernible shapes – marching with purpose, their heads down to avoid the elements, their coats still projecting the red hue that Brother Hawk had already gotten to know all too well. Several of the Redcoats sat proudly atop large, brown horses. These men carried rope that strung back for several meters, looping into a row at least a half-dozen men, women, and children in tattered clothing.

Suddenly, lightening crashed into the clearing – so close that Brother Hawk could feel the static charge in his rain-matted feathers. Startled, the great bird scanned the edge of the forest for the nearest sheltered place to rest. Below and to his left, he spotted a tall pine tree. The branches of the large tree reached well into the clearing, a feature owed to many decades of constant and uninterrupted growth. That tall pine would serve him well until the storm passed. As he landed and perched atop one of the longer limbs, Brother Hawk heard the tumultuous sounds of man. Muskets fired in unison as a young girl darted into his realm.

The girl, it seemed, had also heard the thunder of rifles behind her, because she frantically turned her head in the direction of the noise. But she never slowed her pace. Brother Hawk watched as she raced between pine trees, sometimes greeted by the sting of wet pine needles as low-hanging branches scraped across her arms. She covered her face as she ran.

For some reason, despite the elements, the hawk followed, feeling somehow drawn to the girl's plight. She ran blindly for what seemed like miles. Brother Hawk skirted by, above the trees, unseen by the girl below. Eventually, exhaustion seemed to overtake her and she tumbled to the ground, looking at the sky. The great bird swooped in and rested on a branch of a large white pine just above.

After several moments, the girl staggered to her feet, grabbing hold and pulling herself up on the same tree that Brother Hawk had chosen for his latest perch. She leaned against the pine, breathing heavily as the rain continued to pour down all around her.

Several minutes passed before the girl's breathing began to slow. She looked around at the gathering darkness. *She is free,* thought Brother Hawk, but all around he saw peril. Off to the east a wolf pack scavenged for small prey and to the south, several men moved in her direction. *She must move quickly,* he thought. He could see a man running from the red shapes in the direction of the girl. *I must warn her!*

Lucy Killgrew wrapped her arms around herself, trying to retain what little warmth she could, completely unaware of the large bird of prey watching over her until he swooped down and screamed. For the first time in days, she began to weep.

Feeling more alone than ever, she inched her way down

the trunk and sat huddled at the base of the old pine tree. She was tired, frightened, and hungry, but exhaustion finally overtook her, and she fell asleep.

The bird took to the air.

When Lucy awoke, the morning sky was gray and cloudy and a gentle mist from the low-lying clouds hung in the air. Shivering from the cold, she stood up and surveyed her surroundings. Her muscles felt as stiff as cold glass.

Slowly, she massaged her arms, trying to bring some warmth and feeling back into them. She peered into the forest, but could see nothing out of the ordinary. Yet she could not shake a feeling of uneasiness. Had she really escaped, or were the Redcoats looking for her, even now?

Suddenly, there was crash off to her right, and the Tory Lucius Coffin burst through the thicket about twenty-five yards away, an unsheathed knife in his hand.

Lucy screamed and turned to run, but her cold muscles refused to comply, and she fell to the ground as Coffin closed the distance between them, his eyes full of hatred.

Lucy knew this was the end. Coffin would finally have his revenge, and there was nothing she could do about it. She rolled onto her back to confront her attacker but he was already upon her, his enraged face poised over her own, his knife flashing against the gray sky. But all at once he stiffened, grunted, and his eyes filled with pain and surprise. Toppling forward, his entire weight crashed down onto Lucy's body.

For a moment, Lucy was dazed. But as she struggled out from underneath Coffin's body, she saw an arrow sticking out of the dead man's back.

Ignoring the pain in her muscles, Lucy scrambled to her feet and ran into the thick forest. She had escaped the Redcoats, and then Coffin, and was now being pursued by an Indian.

Brother Hawk, having returned from a long, successful hunt and a short night's roost, darted along overhead, following the same path that Lucy ran. He watched as the young girl below him stumbled again through the trees, chased by a tall, slender man carrying a short bow and a quiver woven out of dark cloth. The man wore a kilt-like sarong of blackened buckskin and his feet moved swiftly across the moist, leafy ground. His tanned face was painted for war in a black and red pattern, a combination of dark coastal soil and a berry-based paint.

The girl ran and ran, never giving a thought to direction, until she finally approached a small clearing. This was not good. She knew enough about the ways of the woods to realize that it would not be safe to run out into the open.

Instead, Lucy ran along the edge of the clearing, staying under the cover of the forest. But, as she ran, her foot caught on a root, and Lucy fell to the ground like a sack of flour, her head striking a large stone.

She heard a soft, dull *thud* and felt a sharp pain in her temple as her head hit the stone. Out of instinct, she instantly rose to her feet and again attempted to run. She had only gone a few feet when a searing pain surged through her head. She felt blood trickling down the side of her face, and wave after wave of blackness clouded her vision.

She struggled to focus her eyes, staggering from tree to tree at the edge of the clearing. She knew she needed to stay under the protection of the woods, but just as she turned to move back into the forest, her legs buckled beneath her and she fell again.

But this time, her mind began to drift away, toward the darkness that seemed to be swirling all around her.

Blackness began to fall over her eyes like a curtain. Just before she slipped into unconsciousness, Lucy saw the sky disappear, blocked out by the shadow of a huge Indian and a large bird circling overhead.

In the distance, Brother Hawk spread his wings and lifted into the light wind as the Mohawk gently knelt beside the girl and lifted her into his arms.

She is free, screamed Brother Hawk for all to hear. *She is free.*

Chapter Two

Celestine

Montreal, Quebec, Present Day

CELESTINE DUFORE STEPPED ONTO the stone walkway as she gently closed the door to her home behind her. She welcomed the moist air outside with a deep breath and a warming smile. *It will rain,* she told herself. *Better bring my umbrella.* Reopening her front door, she reached inside and grabbed her umbrella from the stand in the near corner of the foyer. She then straightened up and stuffed it into the red nylon pack that she carried on her back almost constantly.

It was Sunday and, like every Sunday since she was allowed to walk outside on her own, Celeste would make her way to her grandfather's house to accompany him to

Mass.

Turning around, she set her backpack on the ground and rifled through its smallest pocket for her keys. When she had found them, she stood up and locked the front door to her house, checking carefully to make sure that the bolt had taken hold. When she had finished, she gathered up her bag and skipped lightly to the end of the walkway, where she unlatched the gate to the picket fence surrounding her house and stepped onto the sidewalk outside.

Celeste DuFore was a young lady of about fifteen and, at the time, was still getting used to the idea of people calling her a "young lady." An only child, Celeste had been born into a prominent family whose roots stretched all the way back to the first settlers of Canada. The previous two years had been kind to her, having seen her grow rather tall and very pretty. Though she was a little heavier than most girls her age, she was certainly healthy and fit. In the past year or two, she had discovered makeup, and loved to dress in the latest fashion. Lately, the boys at school had begun to take a great interest in Celeste – a situation that she had not quite grown comfortable with yet.

It was a gloomy day, the lumbering, dark clouds making their way across the cool skies of early fall; the distant thunder sounded the approach of an impending storm. The first flocks of Canada geese were beginning to wing their way southward. It was time for them to leave and escape the harsh Canadian winter that they instinctively knew was approaching. The falling leaves carried by the wind had washed the street in a blanket of yellows, reds, and greens. The smell of the changing season and the burning logs in the many fireplaces hung in the air offering a wonderful feeling of peace. It was that feeling that was eventually broken by the tolling church bells in the distance.

Her grandfather's home was not too far and she enjoyed

walking on the sidewalk through the neatly manicured neighborhood. The streets en route were lined with tall red ash trees and the occasional Norway maple – and Celeste always counted herself lucky to live in a neighborhood where the trees were still allowed to grow to their fullest height. The sidewalk that the young lady traveled upon was made mostly of cement, but it did still bear intermittent patches of brick and stone. The homes that made up the neighborhood, too, were mostly made of brick or stone. These large residences glinted with many windows and most of them gave way to handsome, neatly trimmed lawns scattered here and there with errant leaves from the maples and ash. A few blue and white Fleur De Lys and red and white Canadian flags adorned some of the older houses.

"I love Sundays," Celeste whispered to herself.

As she passed a familiar lawn, the young lady saw the hunched figure of a man she knew well. It was Mr. Trudeau. "Bonjour, Celeste. Off to see the old man?" he asked.

Celeste smiled. "Bonjour, Monsieur Trudeau," Celeste said, "You know that I am; and yet you ask me every Sunday."

"Such a wonderful grandchild. He's very proud of you, you know, Celeste?"

As he spoke, Mr. Trudeau resumed his task of gathering together leaves with his bare hands and stuffing them into the large plastic bag he held between his feet. As she watched, Celeste thought about her grandfather. For as long as she had known him, he had always been a stately but loving old man. After serving in the Second World War as an officer in the famed Royal 22nd Regiment, he served on the city's board of development – and had contributed a great deal of his time to the development and maintenance of some of Montreal's greatest neighborhoods and parks. He had always taken great pride in both his heritage and his city, a quality that endeared him to most of the members of the community.

Despite his busy lifestyle, Celeste's grandfather had always spent as much time as possible with his granddaughter. "The apple of my eye," he often called her, filling her with all the warmth of a cozy old Hudson Bay blanket. Over the years, his care and attention showed; Henri DuFore had been instrumental in shaping his granddaughter into the strong, independent, capable young woman that she had become.

"He's my grandfather," Celeste replied proudly.

Henri DuFore was up early that morning. He had not slept very well and thought that he might be coming down with a cold. Whatever it was, he was not quite feeling as fit as he usually did on the mornings he'd get a visit from his granddaughter. He felt empty inside, as if something were missing. *I'm seventy-nine years old,* he thought. *Maybe someone's trying to tell me something.* He mumbled slightly as he looked upward to heaven and rolled out of bed.

The old man hobbled into his den and past the multitude of pictures and photographs on the wall. On one side of the room was his library of new and very old books that had been passed down from generation to generation. Henri DuFore, after all, was the patriarch of the family and, as such, was not only in charge of directing its future, but was responsible for maintaining its past, as well. On the other side of the room sat the fireplace, embers still glowed from the night before. The mantle held an old clock and two framed old black and white photographs. One was of a beautiful, smiling young woman, and the other was a handsome young lieutenant posing quite seriously in his army uniform. Except for the ticking of the clock, the room was very quiet. Mr. DuFore walked to his favorite chair and sat down with a sigh, staring into the glowing ash within the fireplace.

Celeste did not have to knock. Pulling out the key that her grandfather had given her, she remembered how proud she had felt on the day that he had first entrusted her with such responsibility. She entered the foyer, calling to him.

"Grandfather, it's me," she cheerfully shouted.

"In here," he called.

The young lady knew where her grandfather would be, but, still, something felt strange. Grandpa Henri was usually at the door, waiting for his granddaughter's arrival.

Celeste headed down the hall, following the winding path to the den. The narrow hall played host to many doors on either side. A door at the end and to the left opened to a staircase that led up to the second floor of the well adorned home. Above her, Celeste knew that there were five bedrooms, each furnished with beds of varying sizes (gathered together over the years to meet the needs of a home full of children) and antique dressers and straight-backed chairs that had grown rather dusty since her grandmother's death. On the near side of the hallway – through a door that Celeste now passed – was an ornate bathroom, complete with an old-fashioned, claw-foot bathtub and polished-ivory faucets. The next door on the right led to the kitchen, a room with a classic, rather European feel with its tiled countertops, antique icebox, and cherry-wood cabinetry.

Passing through to the opposite end of the kitchen, Celeste finally reached the den. As she knocked on the partially opened door, she could not shake the feeling that something was wrong.

"Grandfather?" she called out.

"Hello, my little one," he said.

Celeste's ever-present smile vanished when she entered the room and saw him. "Grandfather, you're not ready. Aren't you feeling well?"

"I don't think I can make it to church today, Celestine." Aside from pet names, her grandfather always used her full name. Everyone else could call her Celeste, but to Henri DuFore, she was his celestial treasure: A gift from heaven. He never told anyone before and scarcely would admit it to himself, but before she was born he hoped for a boy. A grandson to carry on the DuFore name, a boy he could teach to fish, with whom he could share his stories. That all changed when Celestine came into this world. How he remembered tearing up when he held her for the first time and when her tiny hand grabbed hold of his finger, wrapping herself around his very soul.

"What's the matter?" she asked.

"I'm not sure, dear," he replied. "These old bones maybe just need a rest today."

Celeste noticed that the old man was staring toward the fireplace. She thought that he might have grown a little melancholy sitting in this room with the picture of her grandmother.

"Is it grandmother?" Celeste asked.

"I still miss her," he said. "She was a wonderful woman. But, no, child…I was looking at the painting over there."

It was a portrait of an eighteenth century woman, couched in a very old, richly carved frame. The woman was beautiful. Long black curls trailed from her bonnet. She looked strong and vibrant.

Celeste had noticed the painting before, of course, but she had never really studied it. She was so rarely in her grandfather's den, after all. The young lady had always inherently known that the woman in the painting carried some significance to the family, but she never really thought to inquire about what that significance was. Whoever had painted it had apparently been a master. The shades and colors almost seemed to glow with the kind of liveliness not often confined to a painting.

Mr. DuFore shook his head mournfully. "I was also thinking of the many generations of our family – how they lived and everything that's happened to bring us to this time and place. Did you know that that painting has been in our family for over two hundred years?"

Celeste tried to imagine something lasting for such a long time. Growing up near Old Montreal, she had seen buildings that seemed very old – even the occasional chapel or basilica that had been around since before the French and Indian War – but to have something in her grandfather's house that was that old came as quite a shock to young Celeste.

During the 1700s, she knew, British rule had come to Quebec as she had learned in school. The period also bore the Royal Proclamation, the American Revolution, the Quebec Act, and the Battle of Yorktown. All of these significant points in history had their part in shaping the continent that Montreal stood upon – and the painting on her grandfather's mantle had weathered them all.

"You know, Celestine," her grandfather continued, "there are very few families that can account for all of the distant ghosts of their relatives. Fortunately, our family is one of those few."

"You don't really mean ghosts, do you, Grandfather?" Celeste asked.

"Well, there are different kinds of ghosts, my dear. Some are purely memory. Some ghosts haunt the present with the past. Some tease; some tempt. And then there are those that lay dormant."

"Why do they stay dormant?"

"Why do they stay dormant? Well, maybe it's the lack of knowledge we have about them that stills their distant souls."

"Who was she?" Celeste asked suddenly.

"Who?"

"The woman in the painting." Celeste was now certain that there was something eerily timeless about this work. *Kind of like a ghost,* she thought.

"Look into her eyes, Celestine," Grandpa Henri said. "What do you see?"

The young lady studied the portrait. At first, she felt a deep sense of sorrow, followed closely by an intense desire to know everything she could about the subject of the painting. She could not put her finger on it, but she felt strangely connected to this beautiful but somehow sorrowful woman. Her gaze dwelled a while on the woman's rounded but striking features. Her upturned nose seemed to suggest a childlike wonder that belied her age. Eventually, Celeste settled on the woman's eyes. They were large, dark brown, and definitely seemed more compassionate and lifelike than she had ever seen in a painting before.

"It's as if she's staring directly at me," Celeste finally replied.

"There's something else," Grandpa Henri said. "She's *looking* for something. She's looking beyond us. Do you see it?"

"Who was she, Grandfather?"

"Maybe you and I will stay home today and talk."

"Talk about what?"

"We can talk about the woman in the painting, little one. She was your great, great, great grandmother."

"Do you know much about her?" Celeste asked.

Grandpa Henri brought his long fingers to his face, running them through his gray, stubbly beard a few times. Getting up from his plush armchair, he walked over to the old cherry-oak desk on the opposite side of the room, next to the fireplace. His once proud and tall posture had grown rather hunched in recent years, though he still usually seemed wiry and energetic. He absentmindedly shuffled through some of the papers on the top of the desk before placing them in a long drawer at its base. He then picked up a glass paperweight and tossed it up in the air a few times, catching it flatly with his hand as it came down.

With paperweight in hand, the old man slowly moved back towards his armchair. Before he sat down, he pulled an ornate maroon velvet stool up to the side of his armchair and patted his hand on its rounded top, signaling for Celeste to sit down.

"Not much about her when she was your age, no," the old man said as he lowered himself back into his chair.

"How old was she when this painting was made?"

"Oh, it would have been about the time she came into the family. That was the custom then. She would've been somewhere around twenty, I suppose."

"Where was she born? Here in Montreal?"

"I'm not sure, little one. Her past before that day has always been a mystery to me. Her name was Marie Celestine or at least that is the name she was given. After living many years among the Iroquois, she came to our family from the wilderness."

Chapter Three

Young John

Hudson Valley, NY, September 1775

IT WAS EARLY AFTERNOON when the old Mohawk pushed his canoe from the riverbank. Laden with a rich harvest of furs, he was heading north to his waiting family. *The snows will soon be here*, he thought. There would only be a short time left for hunting. It was Seskehko:wa, September, the time of freshness. He could smell it in the air. The water was cold and still and, save for the intermittent sounds of water dripping from his paddle as he lifted it high with each stroke, there was an uneasy silence all around him.

The Mohawk's name was Young John. The English and French trappers who had known him in the early years had too difficult a time with his real name Kaien Taron Kwen, and so "Young John" was born.

The Indian had thought a lot about his life on his many solo trips into the wilderness – and this time was no different. He knew that he was getting too old for such long journeys and he missed his woman and his daughters.

Young John was of the Mohawk Nation (Keepers of the Eastern Door) and was born in 1718 in the Mohawk Valley of New York.

When the British and French became engaged in a struggle for control of the new world they used the services of many tribes. In 1754 Iroquois leaders met with representatives of the seven colonies in Albany, New York to renew their alliance with the British.

By the time the revolution began, the Iroquois confederacy was the largest military power in North America. The people grew tall and strong, sustained by a healthy environment and diet. They roamed freely, and throughout their vast territory there were trading posts and custom-houses. No one moved upon the territory of the Iroquois without first reporting their destination and purpose. They were the masters of their domain and everyone knew it, including the British and the French. The whites understood that they could not have made nor could they continue to make advancement into the continent without the help of the Iroquois.

But just as the Nation was fierce in battle, so too was it fierce in peace. The Iroquois, after all, were traders and trappers. They bought and sold with the whites and other tribes and duties were rightfully paid to them. Their gainful employment as guides offered the whites protection. War was, to them, an expense -- and Young John knew that if there were another, it would be very different. Now with the colonies warring with the British, his Chief Thayendanegea (also known as Joseph Brant) would more than likely bring men out to fight on the side of the king. He knew that some of the other tribes of the Iroquois Confederacy would support the colonies. Young John was tired of war and did not believe he would be called on to fight. Should the Mohawk become involved in this war, he and many others the same age would be relegated to the hunting, general provisioning and protection of the village.

With each stroke of the paddle, Young John knew that he was getting closer to the main hunting party. It was his habit to venture out from the main group in the hopes of finding some time to search within himself. But, on this day, his growing concern was with the passenger huddled and asleep on his harvest of pelts. He had rescued her from a Huron attacker earlier that day and had no choice but to bring her along. He was already a father, and now he had to adopt the young white girl in leather breeches. He did not know why men were trying to harm her. He did not care. When he first came upon her, her large brown eyes pleaded with him to protect her. At that point, their spirits met and he had to follow the path to its completion. She was now in his charge, his responsibility. And he would protect her with his life, if necessary.

Lucy awoke to the sound of the paddle lightly tapping on one side of the canoe and then the other. She did not move and the man seated in front of her had not noticed that she was awake. She watched him as he studied the water and the banks to both sides. She had no idea who he was or even if she should be afraid. She tried to think back – to make some sense of why she was here – but nothing came. She saw him searching the water ahead, scanning the horizon. Then, she watched calmly as his gaze turned to her.

The long, lined face that stared back at her showed no sign of emotion, but still seemed to carry a deep sense of warmth. It was an oddly comforting look, even though Lucy had never before met the man. Young John was rugged. His tanned, weathered features suggested many years of running, hunting, and slapping past tree branches, and his leathery face was intricately tattooed with multiple designs. He wore a breechcloth with leather pant-legs tied on, stretching down to a pair of well-worn moccasins. His buckskin shirt completely covered his upper body – and, even though he was well concealed, he looked as if chiseled from stone.

For the moment, Lucy directed her thoughts away from the frustrating puzzle of the day's events and tried to make peace with the situation in which she'd found herself. She did not have time to think for too long, however, because her eyelids were growing heavy and her mind was beginning to swim.

Young John searched the way ahead, scanning of any marker or sign of another person. It would be better for him if he were not found carrying the girl. Perhaps it would be better for her, too. He turned back to her warily, hoping to find some sense that she had regained consciousness. Several hours earlier, he had given up trying to talk to his new companion, for she drifted too easily in and out of sleep. This time, when his eyes met hers, though, he could sense that she'd finally come to herself again.

"You've awoken, little one." His words came in a gentle tone, but he returned his focus to the terrain. He had an uneasy feeling that he was being watched.

"Who are you?" the girl asked.

Young John thought that he had understood the meaning of her words. "Kaien Taron Kwen," he replied.

He looked at Lucy squarely and hit his chest with the top of his paddle, repeating, "Kaien Taron Kwen!"

Lucy could make no sense of the Mohawk words and he could see it in her face. He shrugged, and then said, "Yawng Jean!"

"I...I don't understand," Lucy said.

The Mohawk pounded on this chest again, saying "Yawng Jean" several times. He then raised his palm to the air and directed his hand at Lucy, as if to say, "and what's your name?"

The young lady finally understood. Her head had been a little woozy before and it had taken her a moment to figure out what Young John's gesture actually meant.

"I'm..." Lucy paused, her eyes darting from the rounded floor of the boat to the dark, misty waters that ran along the tree line drifting by. A vibrating sense of terror charged through her; what made her think they were being followed? Involuntarily, her hand flew to her mouth and stuffed the aborted scream back in. She needed more than anything to remember her name.

"I...I..." she finally said. Tears filled her eyes.

Young John leaned over and stroked her dark hair for a moment before gesturing for her to lie back down. Too troubled to resist, Lucy settled her head back on the pelts beneath her, still struggling for the best way to respond.

"Do not you worry, little one," Young John said in his native language. *"We'll have a lot of time to reach an understanding. I come from a home up north, and we will be there soon."* Of course, in the lyrical rise and fall of the Mohawk language, 'soon' could have been measured in weeks or even months.

Young John gazed upon the girl in his care, looking at her head wound with concern. Clay-red blood had begun to seep through the poultice that the Mohawk had prepared. The bandage would need to be replaced, and to do that; he would have to find a safe place to go ashore.

Clever as he was fierce, Young John did not care much for the British, the army his nation had backed during the French and Indian war. He was Kaniahkenhake ("People of the Flint"). Of the three Kaniahkenhake clans – Turtle, Bear, and Wolf – Young John had descended from the Bear clan. Maternally driven, the clans were passed down from the mother for centuries. Young John's mother had belonged to the Bear clan too.

He had been raised around the French-speaking whites, and so he spoke French fluently, along with a few words in broken English. His village was comprised of about 100 stone homes, surrounded by the fields and gardens. The design of these homes had been adapted from the French. Whole families lived within their protective walls. Surrounding the village were fields – where corn, squash, and beans (the three sisters) were grown and harvested by the women of the village.

Growing up, Young John's proficiency with a club, bow, and musket was celebrated amongst the tribesmen. He could discharge five well-aimed arrows in under a minute and he always carried a full quiver along with his two primed muskets.

Though the river had many turns, it was still and glass-like, which made the going easy. The sun was lower now, and Young John tried to get as much distance out of this particular day as possible. He had left two men behind -- one white and the other a Huron. For all the Mohawk knew, the brothers of both could be tracking him now. He knew the Huron hunted in groups – and it was a certainty that the young girl's rescue had made him a prime target for revenge.

He did not kill the white man so it was not important,

but the Huron...well, that was another matter. What was a Huron doing in Young John's nation in the first place? The Huron and the Algonquin, as a rule, would not dare trespass or risk a conflict with the Iroquois. Young John resolved himself to the fact that it was just another piece of a growing mystery. But these were questions that would have to wait. Any answers would be forthcoming soon enough.

Because the skirmish took place on the eastern side of the river, he would stay close to the western side. This might just give him some time or an edge. He always looked for an advantage in everything he did in the wild. He was a man of the land. The trees were his protection and the rivers were his guides.

As he gazed at the young girl, he could not help thinking, *why were the whites trying to harm someone so young? Is she of noble birth? More importantly, will other whites come looking for her?*

Lucy stirred once again. Young John brought the paddle in and scooped both hands in the clear water. "Oneka (*Water*). O-nay-ka," he said slowly as he reached forward and poured the cool liquid into her mouth.

"O-nay-ka," she responded.

"*I think maybe we will camp early today, eh little one?*"

He looked at her and smiled. "*Maybe you are hungry, too? Hungry, he motioned rubbing his stomach.*" Katonhkara'ks."

He was speaking to her in French and Mohawk, and Lucy had not understood one word. Even though some of the language seemed familiar, nothing was coming to mind.

Young John knew that the best place to camp was still an hour up ahead; he also knew that the girl needed to be tended and fed. So he steered his canoe to the western bank. The old Mohawk would have to pull into shore before sunset. And that would not be too much longer.

Three well-concealed figures moved among the trees lining the shore, studying Young John's canoe. Stooping low and looking further down the river, they anticipated the best place for the ambush. The three moved away from the shore and ran inland, cutting the distance in half.

Chapter Four

Bigelow Farm

Hampshire, Massachusetts, 1775

WILL ASHLEY RODE UP to the small Massachusetts farm and thought about how accurately Lucy
had described it. The setting was very tranquil -- almost as
if the war had, for the moment, left the area untouched. A
cabin of great, heavy logs stretched well beyond the size of
a typical cabin of the day. Its northern face was lined with a
covered porch, complete with rocking chairs. Mr. Bigelow,
Will could see, had been an expert carpenter. About fifty
paces to the east of the proud home sat a tall and well-kept
barn. The young rider could not see any sign of animals
either inside or out. On the far side of the barn was a thick
patch of trees that had developed as an offshoot to the

forest that Will had just ridden through. The clearing that had formed between the patch and the forest itself was a kind of half-circle, with its mouth opening to a rolling plain of beautiful and uninterrupted land.

Will had hoped that Lucy would have found her way back here. Many times during the journey, he had imagined her running out to greet him as he rode up to the door.

A small, red-haired woman appeared in the doorway. "State your business," she said roughly. "Speak up now. I've no time to be wasting."

"Ma'am, I'm William Ashley," he replied. "Lucy's friend Will."

"You know my Lucy?" came a voice from inside the home.

The red-haired woman moved aside to allow another woman, frail and very pregnant, to step out onto the porch. "You know my Lucy?" the pregnant woman asked again.

"We used to talk when she rode out to Boston to see the Captain. Are you her mother?"

Hope flickered in the pregnant woman's eyes. "Yes, sir. My name is Nancy Killgrew. What can you tell me?"

It was plain to Will that Nancy Killgrew had received too much bad news of late. He had heard they had brought her husband's body back to the farm on the same day she learned Lucy had disappeared. About fifty yards to the left of the house by four newly planted trees, two fresh graves scarred the ground: Captain Killgrew and Peter Bigelow.

Will's eyes dropped to his horse's bridle, unable to meet her gaze any more. "I was sorry to hear what happened to the Captain, Mrs. Killgrew."

"Well, get down from your horse," said the red-haired woman. "I'm Jenny Bigelow – Nancy's friend. You come inside and tell us what you know about Lucy."

"Thank you, ma'am. I *could* use a little rest."

As Will dismounted, he caught Nancy's eyes again, hopeful, frantic. He looked away.

"Tea?" Jenny asked, offering him a chair at the kitchen table.

"Tea would be fine, thank you."

Nancy Killgrew heaved herself into a chair at his side. "What word on Lucy?" she pleaded, wringing her hands over the hem of her apron as she sat.

They must know the news isn't good, he thought. "Well, we're sure she was taken prisoner by the Lobsterbacks, but we can't find out much more than that. Only we spoke to some patriots who reported seeing a British patrol with some prisoners including a young girl heading north. We searched the last place they were sighted, but couldn't find a trail."

The hem of Nancy's apron was twisted so tightly around her hand that her fingers were turning a lurid crimson. "You mean she's just gone?" she asked.

"Well, no, ma'am. You see, some scouts came upon a British patrol and they reported prisoners, but no girl. So it might be that she got away. Or maybe was taken by a different patrol. We just don't know."

"Lucy could always take care of herself," Nancy said eagerly. "My Tom – Captain Killgrew -- saw to that. Remember, Jenny, once Tom left Lucy in the forest for three days with only a knife, a length of twine, and a piece of flint?"

Jenny nodded vigorously. "Yes, I remember you telling me that she came home filthy from head to toe, but she had trapped a rabbit and made stew out of the wild herbs and vegetables she foraged from the woods."

"Well, Mrs. Killgrew, if she got away, she might have

latched onto some of the old trails." Will shook his head. "But that's a lot of territory," he said. *And a lot of hostile territory, as well,* he thought.

Mrs. Bigelow finally returned with the tea. It was stronger than Will would have liked, but he was just happy to have something other than water to drink. Tea was a luxury that he had not been afforded since he joined up with the resistance.

After several long drafts of the warm, chalky liquid, Will Ashley smiled at his host, Mrs. Bigelow. He took notice of the fact that she looked much older than Mrs. Killgrew. Both women, he knew, had suffered greatly in recent weeks. But whereas the smallest vestige of hope brightened Mrs. Killgrew's brown eyes, Mrs. Bigelow's hazel ones looked tired and completely defeated. When she noticed Will's smile, her lips curled in response, but there was no joy in the gesture.

"But if she's all right," Nancy continued plaintively, "she should have been home by now. Can you go look for her, Will?"

"I need to be heading to Newburyport," the young man replied. "I volunteered to join up with Colonel Arnold. Something really big is brewing, and I'm going along with Captain Morgan and his Virginia riflemen."

Both women's faces fell, and Will was not quite sure what to say. The territory where Lucy was last seen was vast and, unless he could find a trail, there would not be much chance of finding her. Of course, even if he could not find Lucy on his own, he might be able to find someone who had seen her.

"Mrs. Killgrew," he said, "wherever we'll be heading, I can make this promise: if I hear or see anything, I'll let you know."

Nancy looked down at her bulging stomach. Will could

tell, even in the dim light surrounding her, that she had grown quite accustomed to crying. After a moment, the proud woman raised her head, a strong conviction in her eyes.

"Lucy wouldn't just disappear, Will. Not if she had anything to say about it. But you go on now and do what you can."

"You have my word," Will said, pushing himself away from the table. "And with any luck, she'll be home before too long."

"With any luck, you'll all be home before too long," Jenny said, standing to lead Will to the door.

Nancy stood too, gripping the edge of the table in pain.

Chapter Five

Ambush

Hudson Valley, NY, 1775

THE SUN WAS ALMOST down when the three Huron realized that the Mohawk was not coming. An angry panic overcame them as they pointed wildly at one another, trying to figure out where their target had gone. They all knew that if they had missed this opportunity, they might never get another one. They knew the consequences of being here. They were on Iroquois territory; they should not be.

"He rides a kenu," said the leader of the trio, speaking in his native tongue. *"How could we lose one warrior in a kenu? There is only one river."*

"*He could have taken to the land,*" said the shortest of the group. He wore a single feather in his left ear, a proud tradition that had been passed down in his family for centuries.

"*Or stopped to rest,*" said the third Huron. He had been a close friend of the man that Young John had killed. The need for revenge broke upon him like spring waters to a beaver dam.

"*Then we wait for the setting sun,*" said the leader, silencing the others with a wave of his hand. "*If he is ashore, there will be firelight to guide us.*"

An hour passed as the three Huron squatted in the brush near the shoreline. The dusk was definitely beginning to deepen. Before long, the leader could see a small glow in the distance.

"*There,*" he said. "*He has made fire.*"

"*Then we go,*" said the third Huron, a wild anger flashing momentarily in his eyes, cutting the approaching darkness like torchlight.

"No," said the leader. "*We wait for dawn. The best spot for the ambush is here. We wait for the Iroquois to leave camp.*"

Young John, in testament to his cunning and awareness, had sensed the impending attack. He had lived through enough battles and bloodshed to know that the Huron enemy never allowed a death of one of their own to go unchecked. Pack hunting was their tradition, too, and the warrior he had killed had certainly been hunting.

It was this feeling of danger – coupled with the blood seeping through the girl's poultice – that had caused him to pull ashore. His fears about the eastern shore had been confirmed earlier, when he thought that he heard his pursuers beating a path through the underbrush on the east riverbank. And so he chose the western side to lay camp.

"You're getting stronger, I think," said Young John as he handed Lucy some dried fish.

The young woman looked the food over, trying with all her conviction to keep from looking disgusted. She could not remember if she'd ever had dried fish before, but she certainly had a hard time believing that she'd ever put anything that looked like it in her mouth. Realizing that not eating the fish would insult her new caretaker; she politely nibbled on the safest-looking end. After another bite or two, she realized that it was both safe to eat and far more delectable than she'd guessed it would be.

"Thank you," she said. "I *am* very hungry."

"You eat your fill, little one," Young John said, pointing at the satchel he had laid on the ground and then rubbing his stomach as though it were full.

Lucy laughed without really knowing why. Something about this Indian made her feel completely at home. *Home.* The thought shot through her like a musket round. She needed to get home. But where was home? A kind of dull screen seemed to prevent all of her significant memories from coming to the forefront of her mind. The ideas were there, she just could not quite make them out. Angry with herself (and a little frightened about the condition of her head), she finished chewing her second helping of fish, gingerly touched the bandage above her left temple, and stretched out in the soft cool grass. Her back rested against a large oak tree. The last vision that she had that night was of Young John blowing on the small fire he had prepared, nervously looking to the eastern shore of the river after each drawling breath.

Dawn was coming up fast when the snapping of a twig

in the distance startled Young John from his sleep. It was all the warning he needed to know that his best course of action would be to head his attackers off before they reached the fireside.

No sense in involving the girl, he thought, reaching for his quiver, bow, and favorite of two muskets. He slung the weapons over his back and softly beat his way south along the river.

After a few dozen paces in the direction of the sound, Young John turned sharply to his right, leading his attackers away from both the river and the little girl in his care. Lucy lay sleeping by the fire that her caretaker had kept going all through the night, blissfully unaware that her life was being saved.

Before long, she stirred, feeling oddly alone despite the fact that she'd been sleeping. When she opened her eyes, her fears were confirmed. Young John had left. Instinctively, she looked for a weapon. The canoe near the shore seemed like the best place to start, so she clumsily crawled inside and began digging through the loose pile of furs. Somewhere near the bottom of the pile, she found Young John's other musket. The young woman carefully checked to see whether it held shot and powder. Satisfied that the gun was loaded, she propped herself up on the furs, her back facing the river, and pointed the gun at the still-dark jaws of the forest.

Running at a swift but quiet pace from the south, the Huron caught a glimpse of their target, as he turned west, away from the river. Bent reeds near the shoreline and strewn branches on the lower-reaching trees guided the pursuers directly along the path that Young John had taken.

"He is so careless," said the leader, gasping through the words. *"He leaves every sign of his direction."* He felt

like screaming in victory, though his heart kept him quiet. Something seemed to be lurking – but it had not quite occurred to him yet that his prey had been leaving clues for a reason. He actually *wanted* to be followed.

Up ahead, silently and carefully, Young John slipped off the path that he had created. He snaked his way back through the underbrush, careful not to leave any signs of his new direction. Heading back in the opposite direction and remaining up wind from where he came, the Mohawk hoped to get the drop on his pursuers as they followed his reckless path to the west.

Back at the canoe, Lucy's eyes grew heavy again. She had gotten so accustomed to drifting in and out of sleep, by that point, that she did not even notice as the background of her vision slowly melted from that of a forest's edge to that of a closed window and an open field. The one constant between her waking sight and her sleeping sight was the barrel of the musket that she still held in her hand. But now, ancient trees had become wind-swept fields and ghosts of familiar-looking men and women. These shadowy figures drifted in and out of her dream-sight.

Lucy felt gripped with fear and a sorrowful anger that she could not quite identify. For a moment, she allowed herself to take her eyes off the dancing shadows and look at the room around her. It, too, was familiar – as though she'd been in it many times before – but she could not remember its significance.

Before she could get too comfortable, she felt her finger tightening on the trigger and turned just in time to see the musket-ball discharge slowly from the barrel and make its way toward the window. Glass shattered and eased its way to the ground. An eternity seemed to pass as the shards scattered all around the dreaming girl. The bullet passed beyond sight, out into the field and in the direction of one of the shadowy figures in front of the house.

The imagined sound of the musket blast in Lucy's dream was followed shortly by the very real sound of a musket blast off to her left. The young woman startled, waking to the sight of her caretaker as the Indian ducked behind a tree-stump and turned to load his rifle.

Lucy watched as Young John tamped the ball down into the powder. As he did so, a Huron came charging out from the underbrush to the south of the scene, swinging a club wildly above his head.

"Look out!" Lucy screamed.

The warning had come just in time. Young John dropped his musket and grabbed his attacker just as the Huron had jumped over the tree stump and begun to swing his club down. The Mohawk flung his enemy into the weeds behind him, seizing the moment of confusion by grabbing the war club and smashing it into the Huron.

With his back turned to the south, Young John did not see the leader of the war party charge in behind him. Before the Mohawk could even gather his musket back into his arms, the second Huron was upon him.

There was a loud crack and a thud behind Young John. The proud Indian turned to see his young companion standing tall, shaking slightly, a smoking musket in her hand. The second attacker lay dead in the muddy clearing.

Lucy stood in shock. Though she had memories of holding a musket – and even dreams of firing one – she had no idea that she was such a sure shot.

The third Huron – the one with the single feather in his left ear – stepped reluctantly into the clearing, his bow drawn limply back. When he saw that the Mohawk had finally scooped his gun back off the ground, he stopped, too frightened to attack and too proud to run. He turned his focus to the girl standing by the Mohawk canoe. She was packing another round into her musket. Without a sound, the Huron turned and bolted back into the woods.

"You fire like a true warrior," said Young John in his native language, proudly grabbing hold of both her arms and she in turn grabbing hold of his in a congratulatory embrace.

Lucy allowed the strange man to draw her near to him. Though she had no memory of him, his fatherly warmth seemed somehow familiar.

"Let us go pack the kenu," said Young John. *"We will be safe now. It will be many days before that Huron is back in his own nation."*

Lucy and the Indian carefully placed their muskets in amongst the furs. Young John pulled the quiver off his back and set it near the front of the canoe, just at the foot of where he would stand. He then motioned for Lucy to get inside before pushing the canoe back into the water and gracefully hopping back onto his perch.

He stood and paddled for a while, confident that his journey could now continue without interruption. After a few long strokes, he noticed the unfamiliar sound of a second paddle in the water. He turned to see that his companion had found the other oar beneath the furs. She was timing her strokes with his, pressing hard along the current as though she'd done it many times before. What felt like fatherly pride swelled in the Indian's chest.

As the canoe sliced through the still water, Young John looked back at his companion and said, "Tekawí:iaks," pointing to Lucy. "Tekawí:iaks." ("She Crosses the River"). For in Young John's mind, she had indeed crossed over the river from her world into his. Lucy knew instinctively that she had just been given a name. Whatever her hazy past would reveal, it seemed – at least for the moment – that she had a future with Young John.

The words had no sooner escaped the proud Mohawk's mouth when Lucy sensed that they were not alone. She turned to see five other canoes drift gracefully near their canoe, the Iroquois hunters looking upon her with profound curiosity. She had no fear because Young John seemed very content at their presence. Young John greeted them all with a silent wave of his hand. The canoes carried the rest of Young John's wayward hunting party.

Chapter Six

Colonel Arnold

Newburyport, Massachusetts, September 1775

WILL ASHLEY WAS RUDELY awoken on his first morning in Newburyport. As his eyes snapped open, he could see that the private who had shaken him awake was not much older than himself. He was aggravated by the rude awakening, but knew that it was time to begin the first day with his new brigade. Being alert when Morgan and Arnold called him to arms would be more important than anything.

"The time for sleep is over, soldier! Prepare to march!" A corporal outside Will's tent barked the orders, but still, he could tell that they'd been meant for him. When he got outside, he could see that his suspicions had been correct. He was the last in a row of tents a mile long to get up and begin packing. Half-dressed men furiously gathered their tent-poles into the canvas they'd been holding up. Others rolled their supplies into huge packs and swung them onto their backs, ready to move.

For some reason, the scene reminded Will of his childhood. He'd been born in a cabin outside of Richmond, Virginia. Growing up in such a place, he was used to camping out under the stars. For Will's eighth birthday, his father had given him a bolt of sailcloth that he had bartered from a friend for some tobacco. Will immediately went to work fashioning a tent. He spent so many nights in that tent that his two older sisters grew jealous. They whined to no end until Will let them use the leftover fabric to make tents of their own. Of course Will was convinced his was the best of them all. The three children would line up their tents in the field behind the house, telling jokes and arguing with Will about whose tent was the best.

As a young boy, Will loved to roughhouse with his friends. They would play soldiers, climb trees, and wrestle and scrap every chance they got. As a result, as he got older, Will never felt the need to turn from a fight. He had grown into a slim and toned young man with hazel eyes and very dark hair. Tracking and hunting had quickly become his two favorite pastimes.

Despite his rugged nature, he was known to read a great deal and contributed intelligently to every town hall meeting. He really enjoyed the heated discussions about the writings of Samuel Adams, Patrick Henry, and Richard Henry Lee that would take place at each gathering.

In 1774, he made his way to Massachusetts at the time and place when discontentment with the British seemed most evident. If there was going to be a scuffle, then he wanted to be a part of it. He enlisted as soon as it became clear that war was about to break out.

For the better part of a year, he marched and fought bravely in several skirmishes. He had seen Tom Killgrew, his first Captain, die in the battle of Breeds Hill. From there, he had marched and traded fire with the British all the way to Newburyport. It was here that he had joined up with Daniel Morgan's Virginia riflemen. Will's sharp eye and sure shooting had been welcome from the moment he arrived. On the first night, he had learned that the company had been personally selected by George Washington to embark on an extremely risky mission.

Will snapped out of his reverie and stretched his arms. Men were moving about in all directions, some faster than others.

"Well, I'll be," came a familiar voice, echoing from across the field. "Will Ashley, as I live and breathe."

Will looked around. The worn canvas tent just to his left swayed, rustled, and then produced a face Will knew well. Will grinned as David Weaver followed Ben White; the first familiar faces the weary traveler had seen in weeks.

"I thought you boys was dead!" shouted Will.

"Naw, Will. We're too dumb to get ourselves killed," said David. "We're here for the duration, I guess."

Laughing, the three friends slapped each other on the back. Will flicked what remained of Ben's left ear. "Ear's lookin' good, Ben. I see the Brits ain't took the other one yet, huh?"

"I have every intention of keepin' it, too," replied Ben. "Hungry? What say we get us somethin' to eat?"

"This way," said David. "Hey Will, whatever happened to that girl we met on the road to Cambridge? Lucy, was it?"

"We've been lookin' for her right along," Ben added.

"We think the British took her," said Will. "Nobody knows where she disappeared to. But I'll tell you this: I'm gonna keep on lookin', no matter where this war takes us!"

Will remembered the day the three of them met Lucy on her way to Cambridge to meet up with her father, Captain Killgrew. She had been riding a captured British horse.

"If you please, sir, do you happen to know a Captain by the name of Tom Killgrew, who is serving with Mr. Knox's Massachusetts troops?" she had asked.

The three young men had quickly exchanged confused glances. Her accent sounded colonial, but then, you could not tell a Tory by the accent. "What's your name, girl?" Will had asked her. "And what're you doin' wearin' buckskin breeches?"

"I'm the Captain's daughter, Lucy Killgrew, and I'm not a girl. I'm thirteen years old, and I'll be called a woman, thank you."

She had taken a deep breath and composed herself, just like the woman she had claimed to be. Then, she had asked politely, "Now gentlemen, if you please, about my father. Do you know him?"

Drums called the men to assemble, wiping Lucy's image from Will's mind – for the moment, at any rate. The three friends fell quickly into line, three long rows of soldiers facing the drums that sounded in the field before them. In a few minutes, the call to march was made and the soldiers proceeded in their rows, following the steady beat that rolled in the distance.

A hundred yards down the stretch, Will passed in front of the command tent. The large, tri-posted structure was well protected. Six guards in reasonably new, blue uniforms stood near the entrance. Inside, Will knew that Captain Morgan, his commander, was plotting strategy for the upcoming battle. What he did not know was that Captain Morgan was consulting with his closest confidant, Colonel Benedict Arnold.

Captain Daniel Morgan stood straight, his shoulders thrown back as he and Colonel Arnold pored over the hand-drawn map spread on the official table in the middle of the command tent. Morgan had not been charged with the command of so many men without reason. He had served with the Colonial forces as early as the French and Indian War. And he had fought bravely – a feat he had repeated more than once in the early goings of the Revolution. George Washington rewarded his valor a few months earlier, when he was commissioned captain of a company of Virginia riflemen.

Benedict Arnold, like Morgan, was a courageous man of great courage and strong convictions. By the time he reached Morgan's court, Arnold had already earned himself the reputation of the romantic and adventurous colonel who commanded by sheer impulse.

When he had heard the news of Lexington, Arnold – then captain of the Governor's Guard – had volunteered the 60 men under his command to attack the British at Boston. Shortly thereafter, the Committee for Safety promoted him to colonel.

Arnold and Morgan were debating the finer points of the final review of a battle plan that had been in the making for several months. Their plan had two purposes. First it called for a two-pronged attack on Canada in order to open a second front and, theoretically, reduce the British military pressure on the fledgling rebel troops in Boston. Secondly, it was hoped that the French population would be so emboldened by the American attack that they might be convinced to fight with the Americans and join up as the fourteenth colony.

"Now," said Arnold, "General Schuyler will attack from New York, here; and then, General Montgomery will take his troops and attack Montreal. Once the city has been taken, he'll join Schuyler and drive through to Quebec."

"It seems like such a long way to go," said Morgan. "I only hope we're correct in trusting that the French population will join us."

"Why wouldn't they? No one wants to live under a conqueror's thumb, Morgan." Arnold hesitated for a moment and then continued. "We'll depart from this place and get ourselves to Maine. Then, we shall boat up the Kennebec and Dead Rivers, here; then, meet up with Schuyler and Montgomery at Quebec."

Morgan rubbed his chin, studying the plan that he had been reviewing for a week. "Twenty days," he said.

"What's that?" said Arnold.

"I was just thinking, sir. Twenty days, and 180 miles. Such a long way." The Captain rubbed his stubbly beard, his brow furrowed with concern.

"Come, come, man," said Arnold. "The men are up to it."

Morgan shook his head. "Well, sir, I'm sure the men can do it," he responded hesitantly. *If the bateaux are ready and where they should be,* he thought.

"Morgan, I've dispatched a scout to Schuyler, informing him of our intention to move out today."

So it was already settled. "Very good, sir."

"Ready the men, then, Morgan," ordered Arnold.

"Yes sir," said Morgan, his salute much more confident than he felt.

Ben had fallen to the back of the line by stopping to pull a sharp pebble from his shoe. By the time he had put the shoe back on and stood up, he was marching alongside Will, one of his best friends since childhood.

"Look who's here," he said, slapping Will on the

shoulder.

"Not so loud," said Will. "I want to hear if they call any orders."

"Orders, nothing. All we gotta do is keep marching until they tell us not to march anymore. Then, we gotta shoot in whatever direction they tell us to shoot in."

"That simple, huh?"

"What? It's harder than that?"

"You mean to tell me that you don't think about the battle plans or how the enemy moves...things like that?"

"Nope."

Will looked into the clouds above him. They were a full gray, but did not appear to be big enough to produce any real rain. One of them drifted in front of the sun just as he looked skyward. *Whatever the orders,* he thought, *I hope they take me to Lucy.*

"How can you fight without paying attention to your orders?" he asked, exasperated.

"I don't know," said Ben. "Just march and march. Point and shoot. Kept me alive so far, hadn't it?"

"Barely," said Will, allowing himself to smile as he flicked his friend's half-ear again.

Eventually, things quieted down some. As the men grew a little more tired, talking ceased entirely. After a few miles of uninterrupted marching, Captain Morgan came charging up on his horse, amidst scattered cheers from some of the older men.

"We march to Maine!" yelled Morgan, almost reluctantly.

Many of the men who had just cheered let out a steady groan.

"How many miles you think that is, Will?" Ben asked, seeing that his friend's shoulders had slumped and that he had begun to walk with his head down.

"I don't know, Ben. Maybe 150. 200."

"Shoot, I remember a time when I walked 150 miles in three days, just to find my sister. She'd gone out lookin' for her horse that'd run off and got herself lost. Well, I put my tracking to work and—"

"You haven't walked 150 miles in your whole life, you liar," said David. He'd seen his friends up ahead of him in line shortly after Morgan had called out the orders and had decided to jog up to join them.

"Have so. You remember that time my sister, Lilly, got lost."

"Yeah, your pa found her in your granddad's farmhouse. And you didn't track nothin', neither. You was just ridin' on the back of your pa's horse."

Will laughed loudly. It felt good to finally take his mind off Lucy – even if it meant listening to Ben's tall tales.

⁂

Later that week, an Indian scout approached a British sentry, who stood guard at his commander's post near a forest clearing. The Indian approached silently, and kept his distance before calling attention to himself.

"Commandant!" he shouted.

"What's all this, then, Chief?" asked the corporal in a heavy British accent, eyeing the native with a disgusted look. The corporal never much cared for dealing with Indians. To him, they were far too savage to associate with civilized men. He considered them to be little more than one of those unfortunate necessities of war.

"Looks like he wants to chat with the captain," said a private, appearing from his post behind a tree when he heard the Indian calling.

"Eh?" mumbled the corporal. "What've you got there, Chief?"

The scout reached into his leather pouch and pulled

out Arnold's letter of dispatch for General Schuyler. The British were now aware that an attack on Canada was imminent.

On September 21, 1775 George Washington advised congress that the plan was in effect.

To Continental Congress:
I am now to inform the Honorable Congress that, encouraged by the repeated declarations of the Canadians and the Indians, and urged by their requests, I have detached Col. Arnold with 1000 Men, to penetrate into Canada by way of Kennebeck River and, if possible make himself master of Quebec....

Chapter Seven

Wilkes

Little Springs, NY, September 1775

AS THE TWILIGHT THICKENED, Wilkes approached the home of a colonist whom he knew to hold the Revolution in his heart. The colonist was an old man who had been celebrated among the townspeople for being well read and wise. As far as they were concerned, it had been unfortunate that the man was so modest (and also too old to fight), for he would have made an excellent statesman in the new world that they hoped to create and a capable soldier in the battle that now raged. His home was near the riverside, to the southeast of where Wilkes had tracked Lucy's final struggle with Coffin.

Wilkes had grown ruthless and was no less hungry for

battle than he had been when he'd first gotten his start as a young man, decades ago. He was born in 1730, just outside of Philadelphia. His parents had immigrated to the colonies two years before they brought Charles Christopher Wilkes into the world. As a child – right up through manhood – he was a loner who did not make friends easily. He was fiercely loyal to King George and had no intension of joining others in denouncing his sovereign. As a young man, he sailed to England to attend military college. Having excelled in his studies, after graduation, he was assigned to the 34th Regiment of Foot. His anger when he heard the news of the French defeat of the British at Fort William Henry in 1757 knew no bounds. Eventually, he was sent back to the colonies to fight as a lieutenant during the defeat of Montcalm in Quebec. Thereafter – because he was not well connected by family or rank – he was regulated to various posts.

The disgraced officer shuddered at the thought of Coffin's body. He had found it more than a week after the Huron arrow had first brought the loyalist down. The light rains and the animals had not been good to Coffin's remains, though they had not managed to wash away all signs of the girl's escape. From the muddy depressions in the grass, Wilkes' expert tracking sense guided him in a western direction, to a small clearing in the woods near the eastern shore of the river. There, he found another body -- this one belonging to a Huron warrior who had been shot in the back with a Mohawk arrow. The many sets of muddy footprints surrounding the body suggested that the Huron had not been traveling alone, though they did nothing to explain why his body had been left behind in such haste.

From a cowering man in a powdered white wig and a stately home, Wilkes learned that the house along the river belonged to a colonialist by the name of Adam Henry. Charged with a new fire of hatred, Wilkes now strode up to the Henry home, the three soldiers in his search party standing nervously at his side, and pounded on the door.

"Yes?" came a voice from inside. "Who is it?"

"It's Corporal Fenning, sir," said Wilkes. "I've brought some wounded men with me. We seek quarter, if you may."

The door creaked open and a stooped old man blinked at his unexpected guests.

Wilkes grabbed Henry by the collar and rammed him up against the surface of his log home. The old man shuddered and winced, dropping the candle that he was holding into the muddy river-soil in front of his doorway.

"Tell me which way he went," barked Wilkes. Behind him, his men stirred, looking very uneasy about attacking such an old man.

"Wh, wh, who?" stammered Henry.

"The one who escaped, my good man. Come on, now. You know. A tall, gangly chap named Fenning!"

"I don't know what you're talking about," said Henry, throwing Wilkes' hand from his collar. "I haven't seen anyone meeting that description."

"It would have been almost two weeks ago. And he may not have been alone."

The old man's shoulders tightened and, for a moment, he seemed to be pondering his escape. With his free hand, Wilkes drew his saber and brought it up to the side of Henry's face, allowing the blade to scrape lightly across the surface of the old man's cheek, like a razor.

"You have thirty seconds before we torch your home and everything inside it," said the officer.

"No...Please. My wife is inside."

"Then I suggest you give me the information I seek,

old man."

"Listen to him, Henry. He's serious," said the corporal at Wilkes' side.

Wilkes turned and gave the soldier a long and threatening look for spoiling his entertainment. "I don't recall giving you permission to speak, Hamilton," he said. Then, turning back to Henry, he could see that the threat had done itself justice. The old man was moments from cracking.

"He passed through here last week. Wednesday, I think it was. He..he now lives in a house that once belonged to his father."

Wilkes' mood lightened a little. *Finally,* he thought, *the break starts to fall my way.*

"And he took to this home?" he asked, his face barely an inch away from Henry's now.

"Yes...yes!" pleaded Henry.

"And how long ago did you say that was?"

"About a week. Maybe more."

"And where can we find the gentleman's residence," Wilkes said in a mockingly cordial tone.

"It's about three miles downriver. On the eastern shore... near the bend."

Wilkes turned to the corporal at his side, a sneer forming on his lips. "We ride along the western shore, Hamilton," he said. Then, he turned back to Henry, easing his grip and straightening up, an insincere smile spreading across his face. "I'm wondering, sir...can you tell us of a shallow place for our horses to wade across the river?"

"Not after these rains, no. You'll have to go to the jetty. It's two miles upriver."

Wilkes balked at the idea of having to waste so much time traveling two miles in the opposite direction. In a moment, though, he calmed his frustration and returned his gaze to Henry's dull, listless eyes. "I thank you, sir. And the King thanks you." Then, turning to the two young soldiers standing behind him, he motioned to the torches that each carried, an evil smile etched into his face. "But the King does not forgive," he said, turning back to face Henry. "Show this man the King's wrath, Private."

The youngest soldier reluctantly approached the Henry home and made to throw the torch into the uppermost window. Before he did, Hamilton said, "Hold, private."

Hamilton was a Corporal and a loyal soldier. Under normal circumstances every officer's orders must be obeyed without question. Hamilton, however, was a man of conscience. No one had to tell him what was the right thing to do; it was as natural to him as breathing. Yet this mission sullied him as a man and as a soldier. He looked at Wilkes with a pleading eye.

Wilkes was oblivious. "Now, Private," said Wilkes, almost laughing.

"Elizabeth!" called Henry, "Get out of the house!" The old man staggered up near his doorway and was almost plowed over by his large wife as she came barreling out the door, dressed for sleep. "Oh thank God," said the old man, though his relief was short-lived. As he hobbled out to the edge of his yard, near the riverbank, he turned to face his once lovely home. With his arm around his crying wife's shoulders, he watched as the fire spread through the upper rooms and then came billowing down the stairwell, framed by the still-open doorway that led into the front hall. He turned to scream at Wilkes, but the British soldiers had already gone.

Further down the road Wilkes thought intently on what had just taken place. He was not sure at that point whether he could count on Hamilton much longer.

Chapter Eight

The Three Sisters

Mohawk Valley, NY, September 1775

THE FIELDS WERE BEING stripped bare of the corn, beans, and squash needed for the long winter ahead. As staples of the Iroquois diet, these nourishing foods had come to be known as "the Three Sisters". What was not immediately needed or what would be held for trade with other clans or the whites was carefully stored for the winter.

As Young John's hunting party came home to their village at last, Lucy noticed the many solid, well-maintained houses that dotted the landscape. A strong home, she knew, meant a strong family. Where that wisdom had come from, however, she was not sure. A man had spoken the words to her as a child; but who was that man? And where was he now?

Made from stone, these well-built homes offered both protection from the advance of man and shelter from the harsh winter elements. As Young John and his party led Lucy closer to the village, she saw many men and women busy with the harvest, some of them out gathering the crops and some of them near the houses, packing beans into bags and lining squash in the shade. The sun was high in the sky when Lucy passed through the entrance of the Mohawk village with Young John. Men and women alike stopped what they were doing to watch with curious eyes the young white girl in buckskin. She was not bound and walked beside a trusted and wise member of the community. There were boys playing a strange sort of game short distance away. The game required them carrying netted sticks catching and throwing a round object. The young girl, it seemed, was not important enough for them to interrupt their game.

Young John walked with Lucy to the middle of the village, where he greeted the gathering villagers. *"I have found this girl,"* he said. *"She has no place to go, so I will allow her to stay with my woman and daughters."*

Three people stepped forward from the small crowd: Young John's wife, Konwáhne; beside her, the eldest of his two daughters Kana Kó:re. She was a little older than Lucy, but not by much. She looked Lucy up and down before smiling and pushing the youngest daughter, Kawehnákens, toward Lucy. The little girl giggled as she moved to Lucy's side. Lucy could not have understood the significance of the closeness, but Kana Kó:re did. It meant that it was now Lucy's responsibility to care for her young sister.

Konwáhne starred at Young John, but said nothing. She stepped toward Lucy, then took her hand and placed it in the hand of her youngest daughter. Lucy instinctively took hold.

Young John, his family, and the villagers continued to speak in their own language, and Lucy stood with her new sisters, confused. She did not understand what anyone was saying. While her past remained a mystery, she was certain that she had never been in a place like this one before. She did not know how to react to the stony and proud-looking woman standing before her.

She was acutely aware of everyone's eyes upon her, and she was not sure what to do. Kana Kó:re stepped forward and stood between her mother and Lucy. Looking Lucy in the eyes, she grabbed Lucy's hand and put it into her mother's. More than anything, Lucy knew that she just needed a warm and safe place to say until she could remember who she was and where she came from. She was grateful for Young John's kindness and wanted very much to show a similar kindness in return. With all that in mind, Lucy looked to Young John, who motioned to her to go with his wife.

Konwáhne reached out her hand, forcing what looked like a smile as she led Lucy (with her youngest daughter still clutching her hand) toward their house. Kana Kó:re looked inquiringly at her father, who remained expressionless. She could almost feel the other girls in the village staring at her. Kana Kó:re turned, embarrassed, and followed her mother, sister, and the stranger.

Lucy's anxiety grew as she felt the hot gaze of the entire village upon her back. She was not sure what she would find in the stone house but, either way, she could not wait to get inside, away from prying eyes.

When the group finally entered the doorway, Lucy was amazed. Inside the home was a large room with blankets, skins, and furs placed along the walls. The cooking area surrounded the fireplace with pots and utensils nearby. At night, the blankets and furs could be made into beds.

Konwáhne gestured for Lucy to sit down. *"You rest,"* she said, helping Lucy out of her muddy and travel-worn boots. *"Kana Kó:re, bring some food,"* she commanded to her eldest daughter.

Lucy studied her new caregiver as she carefully helped her into a fur-lined cot in the corner of the great room. She wore a long frock of a gray fur that Lucy could not identify, already dressed for winter despite the lingering warmth in the air. Her hair was the blackest that Lucy had ever seen and appeared to be every bit as rough and rugged as her husband's. Her clear dark eyes suggested an intense but grave kindness. She had clearly weathered many years of hardship, long journeys, and trying times.

The younger of the two daughters, Kawehnákens, was about 4 years old. She wore long reeds in her braided hair. As the mother bent over to kiss her youngest daughter on the forehead, Lucy could see for the first time the love that existed within the family. For some reason, the sight filled her with a sense of overwhelming joy – a sense that she somehow felt had come from her recent past.

Kana Kó:re returned, carrying some corn-flour bread and syrup. Lucy could see from the expression on her face that she was only doing as her mother had asked and really had no desire to wait on her new companion. The girl was quite pretty, looking very much like a young version of her mother – though Lucy could see a bit of Young John in her strong brow and compassionate eyes – and was almost certainly the same age as Lucy. She was solid and strong, the work-weary muscles in her arms going slack as she set the plate down next to Lucy.

Lucy was not hungry, but she had learned from the weeks on the trail with Young John that it was impolite to refuse food. She accepted with an awkward smile. "Merci," she said softly.

"Merci," said Kawehnákens, smiling broadly and rocking back and forth on the balls of her feet. "Yawekon," she said, rubbing her tummy.

By that point, Young John had taught Lucy enough of the language for the girl to know that the little girl was saying that it tasted good.

"Hen'en...yes," Lucy replied.

Lucy learned many words and phrases from Young John and, now, she could see that the language training had begun again.

That evening, just as with all the others on the trail, Lucy dreamed of familiar yet unrecognizable images. Muffled sounds echoed through her mind. She saw the image of a strange man approaching her. Lucy could not make out the details of his face, but could feel his rage bearing down upon her. She turned to run but instead felt herself falling; the man lunged forward and white flashes burned her eyes. Suddenly the blurred image jerked to a stop, and then the man grabbed her shoulders for support as they continued to fall.

Lucy woke with a jolt. Sweat covered her face and neck. She turned and was startled to find little Kawehnákens sitting beside her. The girl broke into a concerned smile and reached her tiny hand out to wipe Lucy's brow.

Through the large doorway behind the little girl, Lucy could see the sun just coming up in the distance. Kawehnákens beckoned for Lucy to rise. A crisp, autumnal air rushed into Lucy's nose as she sat and surveyed her surroundings. Many of the cots inside the house were now empty, the blankets and top fur neatly stacked as though no one had touched them during the night. Lucy could smell the familiar odor of a fire burning just outside the doorway.

She took Kawehnákens' hand and allowed the little girl to lead her outside. Dew still clung heavily to the grass, soaking and chilling Lucy's bare feat from the moment she stepped into the square field connecting Young John's house to all the others. The sunlight glinted off the dew, lending a twinkling effect to the soft, untouched hills to the east of the village. The firelight danced in a pale yellow in front of Lucy as she followed the little girl's example and sat on a wide log that had been placed in the grass.

Konwáhne was preparing the evening meal and the food that she had suspended over the fire smelled delicious as anything Lucy could remember. Lucy would find that her daily routine would consist of taking care of the young one, a chore that she would come to enjoy. She would also be required to study medicine – a process that consisted of learning about the different roots and herbs and attending the gardens in the spring.

Ash Creek, NY

John Fenning was making some repairs to the north side of his small home when he saw the five riders approaching from a distance. They looked a little ragtag, but were too far off to make out any faces. He thought to himself, *Been captured, escaped…no, sir, no…I been captured and I served out my enlistment with the militia and I'm not goin' back.*

Far off on the hillside, Charles Wilkes led his small band of disguised countrymen in the direction of a man he knew he'd been hunting for days. On the mission with him were a few privates and Corporal Hamilton. One of the privates had served with Wilkes many times and followed him around like a camp dog. His name was Fitzwater, a man with a dubious history and a red eye patch.

John Fenning, one of his remaining escapees, would

have probably forgotten his captor's face by now. Wilkes was counting on it, in fact. There was a kind of sick pleasure that came along with seeing the face of his victims at the moment they learned who he was. *Fenning will be no different,* he thought.

If Wilkes thought he was forgettable, however, he underestimated himself. His face was striking, appearing as though it were chiseled from rock. His piercing gaze was rarely broken by friend or foe and a mere quiver of his lip, lately, seemed to be quite enough to stir even the toughest of his men to action. His right cheek bore three long battle scars and the other side of his face, just beside his left eye and running down to his jaw-line, was carved with a jagged scar from a wound suffered during a saber duel. He had won the fight – as he did almost every fight; every fight, in fact, except this one.

And it was certainly a loss, at least in the way that he considered it. The escape of a prisoner under his watch was no less embarrassing than losing a battle. This particular escape, too, had been especially embarrassing. Although no one would be so foolish as to disrespect him openly, he sensed that, behind his back, the enlisted men in his brigade had been mocking him for allowing such a significant escape to take place. What was worse, they seemed to think him a coward for not pursuing his escapees.

Eventually, he grew tired of the whispered jibes from the men. He begged his commanding officer for a leave of absence with the purpose of vindicating himself of the shame he had brought upon himself, his company, and his country.

"Only four?" Wilkes' commanding officer had asked.

"Just three men and a girl," Wilkes replied.

"All right then, find them and bring them back for punishment."

"Thank you, sir."

It rankled him to show such servitude to an officer half his age, but Wilkes had earned his post – or, rather, a promotion. With his success in battle also came a kind of ruthless indignation toward the enemy, and it was something that the King and his civilized court encouraged. Wilkes was on the verge of a promotion before the escape had occurred. The moment word got out that he'd allowed so many prisoners get away; the papers went unsigned. Wilkes was to remain a lieutenant.

"I will find them, sir. I assure you."

"Well, remember we have a rebellion on our hands, so do not tarry."

"No, sir."

And now Wilkes was bearing down on a weather-beaten shack that he knew to serve as the home of his second-to-last fugitive. It had taken a great deal of convincing to find out from the local colonists just where Fenning lived. He eventually got additional information he needed from a high-society woman with British leanings. He'd even managed to secure some old clothes from her dead husband – the perfect disguise to help get the drop on Fenning.

This one will be easy, Wilkes told himself as he felt his horse's long, black mane flick against his tense forearms. He leaned forward in the saddle and brought his hand back to brush the handle of his saber, more anxious than ever to get to his quarry as quickly as possible.

It's the girl who will give me the most trouble, he thought. Lucius Coffin, before he had gone charging off into the wilderness, had told Wilkes about what a headache Lucy Killgrew could be. When the soldier failed to return, his warnings had been confirmed.

As the mounted horsemen drew closer, Fenning got

his first glimpse of the man leading the pack. His mind strained to figure out who this person was. "I know him," he whispered. "I know…"

Suddenly, shock overtook him. He gripped his hammer tightly in his hand, as though ready to charge into battle with it, but his body froze at the thought. He knew that he had to do something quickly, so he ran inside his house, where he kept his musket. He cursed himself when he found that he'd forgotten to load it again. Keeping an unloaded gun, he knew, was about as useful as a three-legged pony.

His hands trembled as he leaded the powder and ball. Stepping back outside, he cocked the rifle, but it was already too late. The men following Wilkes already had him in their sights. The three riders fired in unison, all of them still charging forward on their horses as Wilkes brought his saber down.

Fenning felt the ball tear through him and he slumped down onto his knees. A rush of cold barreled through him as he looked down at the grass.

"And now to the girl," said Wilkes, a sneer forming across his grizzled face.

In truth, Wilkes had not seen the men escape his column almost two weeks prior, but he could see the girl clearly in his mind as she darted into the forest. It was the last thing he saw before his horse inexplicably reared up and threw him into the mud, like some jester.

Lying in the mud with the rain pelting down upon him, Wilkes was stricken with a mixture of embarrassment and pure rage. He concentrated all of his anger on the sight of the girl and instantly transferred every ounce of vengeance within him on to the thought of her death.

In a moment, a corporal in his charge approached him. He was short and stocky and looked rather like a jester himself in his pressed white vest and long, red coattails.

"Shall I order the men to pursue her, Sir?" the corporal asked.

Wilkes was standing now, his red and white uniform covered with mud.

The officer looked into the woods for a moment, and then looked up at the blackening sky. For some reason, his anger dissipated. He felt assured that the elements would take out his revenge for him. However, the next words out of his mouth would come back to vex him.

"No," he said, "That Yankee girl won't last the night in those woods. Let the rain and Indians have her, and then let the wild animals take what's left. We've got our orders, and we don't have time to go looking for one girl."

Wilkes could not have foreseen just how embarrassing the day would be and how it would follow him around like flies to a horse. The more he thought on it, the more he was determined to find the girl, no matter how long it took. He hoped to enlist the aid of a Huron tracking party he had used from time to time in the past. They were unafraid to venture into unfamiliar or hostile territory and their bravado had served him well. Wilkes had been unsuccessful in locating them for his current purpose. Then he remembered the Huron lying next to Coffin and then thought no more on their whereabouts or their fate.

Chapter Nine

Autumn Moon

Mohawk Valley, NY, November 1775

WINTER WAS DRAWING NEAR and the French Canadian hunting party was heading home. With Washington's two-pronged attack on Canada, the first army under Montgomery was laying siege to Fort St. John's, which protected the approach to Montreal. So far, it seemed, the plan was proceeding as designed.

Just as in every year before this one, they anticipated a fine hunt in Iroquois territory and stopped for some light bartering at the Mohawk village. They would have to make their stay in the village a brief one, as they were not sure if the Americans would succeed or fail. In any event, the men really wanted to be home with their families.

Emile DuFore led the pack of hunters and trappers. Like so many others in his position, Emile had trapped and traveled many miles over the years. His familiarity with his profession projected a strong kind of confidence, as did his steady gaze and thick, dark hair. By this point in the journey, the almost constant stubble on his face had grown into a full beard that, if anything, seemed darker than the hair on his head. He was a lean man with slack shoulders, but he rode proud and high on his horse, lending him an air of quiet dignity. Behind him on his horse rested at least a dozen large furs. In his hand, he held the reins of another horse that trotted slowly behind his own. The second horse's only charge was another pile of furs even larger than the one behind Emile.

This year, for the first time, Emile had brought his son Simon along on the journey in the hopes of training the boy to learn the ways of the wild. To look at him, one never would have guessed that Simon was his father's son. In fact, strangers would have likely assumed that this boy was either a hired hand or, at most, a nephew of the man in his charge. That assumption was very rarely held for too long, however, as Emile was always quick to point out that Simon was his son. Emile, after all, was a very proud father, though he never showed it directly.

Simon was the spitting image of his mother, in truth. His blonde hair and green eyes fascinated the Mohawks in the villages he and his father visited. At 16, he was already taller than his father, too. The fact that almost all of his height came from his lanky legs caused him to look rather short in the saddle, though.

As the hunting party drew nearer the main path that ran through the middle of the village, Simon felt a little awkward. All this was new to him, after all, and being around so many Iroquois made him tense.

Meanwhile, Young John was busy stringing line for a bow that he had just fashioned from a felled tree he had found earlier in the week. The wood had looked dry and almost dead, but had proven to be quite sturdy and strong. This particular bow was not his best work, but he knew that it would be sufficient for teaching his new daughter how to shoot just as he had shown Kana Kó:re. He thought on his daughter's expertise and hoped they would be friends soon enough and she would show the newest member of his family the ways of the bow.

As the Mohawk wedged the head of the bow between two large rocks in the ground and began to draw the two ends of the bow together, he looked to the horizon. As the sun drew near the land, it projected many long wisps of purple and orange against the backdrop of the lazy clouds of the dusk. Before the sunset was a band of silhouettes in the shape of riders.

Normally, this would have startled Young John, as he knew that all members of his tribe were in close quarters for the night. But the speed in which the riders approached suggested to him that they were not here for a fight.

As the riders drew up to the edge of the village, Young John began to walk in their direction. In a matter of moments, he could see that he had been right not to worry.

Ah, DuFore, he thought. *I've been waiting for your return.*

Apart from hunting, Young John's favorite pastime was trading with the whites within his realm. There was something very satisfying about exchanging goods that he himself had worked so hard to attain for goods that he could never have made on his own. Plus, he knew that the act of trading seeded goodwill between the Iroquois and the French and, sometimes, even the English.

Just before he opened his mouth to speak a greeting to his old acquaintance, Young John was struck with a notion that charged upon him like a wild horse. DuFore was a white. Tekawí:iaks was a white.

Maybe, he thought, *it would be best for everyone if I sent Tekawí:iaks away with her own kind.*

Whatever logic he may have felt in the thought was brushed instantly to the side as the Frenchmen approached. While Young John knew DuFore, he would never be totally confident that turning over Lucy to the Canadians was the right thing to do. He felt inside that the girl needed the strength that only he and his village could provide. Time would take care of the rest.

On the edge of the village, Lucy was getting a very different kind of training in the form of learning how to raise a child. Since her first day with the tribe, she had been left to care for young Kawehnákens. And although the girl was quite a handful, she was kindhearted and had respected Lucy even from the very beginning. In fact, more and more, Lucy was beginning to feel like part of the family – though things were still a little rocky with Kana Kó:re.

Lucy was learning the Mohawk language very quickly and had just finished counting to twenty in Mohawk (a lesson that Konwáhne had just taught her on the previous day). She turned and opened her eyes, yelling, "Here I come," into the sky and walking slowly toward a nearby huddle of stones. It was a game that Lucy had taught her new younger sister almost immediately and it was one that Kawehnákens was always ready to play. While the little girl was exceptionally good at hiding (especially considering how small she was), she was not particularly good at keeping herself hidden. Almost always, Lucy would find her young sister as soon as she heard Kawehnákens giggling uncontrollably at the sound of her approach.

This occasion was no different. Lucy rounded the pile of rocks and headed towards a bushel of corn propped up against the wall of the nearest stone house, she began to stomp her feet loudly. The moment she did so, a low and soft string of laughter could be heard coming from behind the bushel. Kawehnákens had an infectious laugh – and Lucy could not help but giggle herself every time she heard it, even though she wanted nothing more than to sneak up on her little sister and scare her out of her hiding place.

By the time Lucy reached the bushel and found Kawehnákens, both girls were laughing loudly.

Kawehnákens bounded out of her hiding spot and gave Lucy a light tap on the shoulder, saying, *"You found me again! Always so fast!"*

"I told you. You always laugh, silly," Lucy said, her Mohawk much improved.

Kawehnákens hugged her new older sister and smiled broadly.

Just as she heard the little girl say, *"Again! Let's play again!"* Lucy turned her eyes toward the entrance to the village and saw the line of strangers atop their strange horses. The village was so large and Lucy had been so occupied with her little sister that she had not seen them arrive.

"Tekawí:iaks," Young John called from behind.

Lucy turned as he walked up to her. He handed her the bow he made along with a full quiver of arrows. "Kana Kó:re....teach." He said as he walked away.

"Thank you," she said feeling a little surprised. *If Kana Kó:re was going to teach her the way of the bow, she thought who was going to tell Kana Kó:re?*

She looked again at the strangers. Always in the mood

to see new things, Lucy wrapped the bow and quiver over her shoulder then grabbed Kawehnákens by the hand and dragged her towards the men just as they seemed to be turning to leave.

As the French were leaving, Emile caught a glance of the white girl looking very warrior like with her bow and all, except of course for the little one tugging away at her arm. Lucy walked with Kawehnákens across the compound and examined the strangers on her way to the gathering. With their pale skin and soft, rounded features, they were like her in some ways and different in others.

"Kawehnákens," Lucy said, turning to her sister, "go to the house. I will be there soon."

Lucy spoke with mix of English and Mohawk. The little girl did not quite understand her new sister's words, but after watching her point to the house several times, Kawehnákens got the meaning.

After giving Lucy a glare, Kawehnákens ran off toward home as Lucy turned and walked the rest of the way to the group of frontiersmen. She was downwind and could smell the pelts they carried – to say nothing of the men themselves.

"And who is this?" Emile asked as he noticed the young maid approaching.

"I am Tekawí:iaks," Lucy replied.

"No, no," he said. "Your accent is strong." He said in English. "You are Yankee. What is your name?"

Lucy frowned. She had struggled long and hard to determine any of the details about her past, but the idea that she had an English name still seemed odd to her. As far as she was concerned, the only name she knew was Tekawí:iaks. Everything else before her Mohawk name was a blank slate, empty and without meaning.

"Tekawí:iaks is the only name I know," she said. "I'm

not sure of anything before my father Young John."

"Well, surely you were not born here," Emile said, looking the girl over.

"No, I was not. I don't remember much before I got here, though."

Emile shrugged. He had seen this before. *Memory is gone,* he thought. *I guess I cannot blame her. Being taken by Indians...must be terribly frightening for a young girl like her.*

The truth was that running into young white girls without memories was not a new experience for Emile. He had journeyed many miles in his time and had been to the gates of many tribes. In his travels, he had come across many whites – women and young girls, mostly – whom the Indians for one reason or another had taken. Almost all of them had no memory left of their lives amongst the whites. Emile usually chalked the memory loss up to fear. Trauma like being taken from one culture and thrust into another, he reasoned, was probably enough to do anyone in.

Emile took great comfort in the fact that this one – this Tekawí:iaks – looked as though she belonged. And she was certainly treated well.

"I shall call you Marie," Emile said.

"Marie?" Lucy asked, slowly forming the name as though it was the strangest sound she had ever heard in her life.

"Yes, the name they've given you here is too hard for me to pronounce. Besides, Marie was my mother's name. It's a fine name. So I shall call you Marie."

Lucy smiled at this silly but friendly man. "Marie," she said, grinning at the sound of it.

Lucy then looked over at Simon, the boy about her age who was riding the horse next to Emile's in the proud line. She was immediately taken with his boyish good looks and felt herself blushing for reasons that she could not quite identify. For some reason, this boy seemed familiar to her – as though she had known him in a former life. Whatever the case, she felt an overwhelming desire to spend more time with him.

"Are you staying?" she found herself asking.

"No, young one," Emile said, touching Lucy's nose. "The season waits for no man...or girl for that matter."

Lucy's heart sank. Whether she would get a chance to spend time with the boy next to Emile or not, she would have enjoyed the excitement of the company of these strangers. At the very least, they were interesting and different – and somehow familiar. Like ghosts from the past.

"And so, Marie," said Emile, "we will leave you now and head home to Montreal. Maybe we shall meet again when we come by next year, eh?" He then looked at Simon. *"Say goodbye to Marie. Where are your manners, boy?"*

Simon had stood by in his saddle all the while, fascinated by this girl. This encounter was so unexpected. He was immediately drawn to Lucy's big and sorrowful eyes. Her long, rough hair and solid form represented the kind of untamed beauty that he had never before seen in Montreal.

The boy found himself searching desperately for the proper words to match his father's demand. He knew that he needed to say "goodbye" and that the beautiful girl standing before him was now going by the name "Marie," but he could not seem to form those two thoughts into a proper sentence.

"Good...goodbye, Mar-Mar-Marie," he finally said. Despite the stammering, he would have been comfortable with the way things had gone, except that his voice had cracked as he spoke, causing Lucy to smile. Feeling a little

embarrassed, he joined up with his father. Simon could feel the heat from his blushing face as he moved next to Emile. He could see his father staring at him from the corner of his eye, but pretended not to notice.

Emile smiled and slightly shook his head. "Do not worry, my son," Emile said. "I saw the way she looked at you. She probably did not even notice your stutter."

Simon could feel the heat rising in his face once again as he rode off with the rest of the men.

Lucy watched with a heavy heart as the half-dozen men wheeled their horses around and slowly rode into the gathering darkness. No matter how hard she tried, she could not shake the thought that these men somehow held a key to at least a portion of her past. At the very least, they all looked and acted just a little more like she did.

Though her life with the Mohawk was a pleasant one, she longed to learn how the whites lived. What's more, she felt compelled to learn more about the boy who had arrived with Emile. She had never even learned his name. And the thought that she would have to wait another year to find out was almost unbearable.

Chapter Ten

Sons Of Erin

Fort St. John, Canada, October 1775

AS FAR AS GENERAL Richard Montgomery was concerned, things were not going well. He had held siege to Fort St. John's for a month; yet the nine hundred men within the fort would not give in, and he needed to break through and take Montreal as quickly as possible. He had considered leaving a small force to maintain the siege, but he would settle on nothing less than a solid victory. The fort was well defended and there had been many skirmishes. The loss of his men had to be kept to a minimum if the eventual attack on Quebec was to succeed. Therefore charging the fort was not an option that he would even consider. His only option was to wait it out and hope that desertions and the food supply would run out.

The weather was becoming colder; the sight of his men milling about the camp shaking the chill from their bones was intolerable to him. It was the indecision of it all that bothered him. The attack on Quebec called for him to join up with Benedict Arnold in a joint force effort.

Richard Montgomery was born on December 2, 1736 in Swords, Ireland. He was the son of a member of the British Parliament and an officer in the British Army. In 1772 he sold his army commission and moved to New York and bought a farm at King's Bridge (Bronx). He was elected to the New York Provincial legislature and being a brilliant tactician, joined in the Revolution and was commissioned Brigadier General.

On the other side of the fort wall was his opponent Sir Guy Carleton, the governor of Canada and with him about nine hundred men. He knew that the loss of this fort would open the way to an undefended Montreal and through out the siege did his utmost to rally the men and keep spirits high.

Born September 3, 1724 in Strabane, Ireland, he was sent to Canada in 1759 and fought in the battle of Quebec defeating the French on the Plains of Abraham. He served as Lieutenant Governor and then as Governor of Quebec Province. He nurtured better relations between the British and the French Canadians, which led to the passage of the Quebec Act. It was a brilliant move on his part and even more so on the part of the British government because the act had done exactly what it was meant to do. The Quebec Act restored the former French civil tradition for private law, which had been ended in 1763 and allowed for their Catholic faith to be practiced. The oath to King

George III made no reference to the British protestant faith and the Act allowed the French Canadians to participate in government. Now, with most of the British troops in Canada fighting the rebellion in the colonies, the majority of the troops at Fort St. John's were French Canadian.

~*~

To the east, there was no glory in Arnold's march through the dense hinterland of Massachusetts. Everything seemed against him as well: the weather, illness, exhaustion and hunger were the enemies now. Freezing rain fell incessantly as they hacked their way through the thick forest.

They had left Fort Western the previous week after picking up the boats (bateaux) they would use on the rivers. Because Washington ordered the boats to be constructed in fifteen days, the builders used green wood instead of dry. Green wood was heavier and made carrying the boats from river to river difficult and dangerous. To add to the difficulties, the flat-bottomed boats could not be rowed; they had to be pushed by poles. Will, David and Ben were on one of the boats manning the poles, struggling to push the heavily laddened boat upstream against the current.

The going was slow. The portage over land to the next river was even slower. There were eight to ten men to a boat made even heavier with supplies. Will's shoulder was straining under the weight of the boat, struggling with every step to maintain a solid footing, counting down the time until his relief would step in. He was close to the front of the column and could see dozens of men hacking at the thick underbrush clearing a path. Gingerly stepping over small fallen trees and having to go around larger ones, the effort was taking its toll. Smaller, older, or wounded men walked alongside, picking up any supplies falling from the top of the boats. Some of the supplies tumbled over into the water and floated away with the current.

Suddenly Will noticed the boat ahead start to shake. The men underneath tried desperately to maintain balance when two men tripped. The boat came down with a dull thud, crushing the two men beneath it.

Chapter Eleven

Ahentáken

Mohawk Valley, NY, October 1775

HIS NAME WAS AHENTÁKEN of the Turtle Clan. He was sixteen winters when the clan mothers had agreed that he would be suitable to be with Kana Kó:re when the time was right.

On the surface, Kana Kó:re did not seem to agree with the clan mothers about this decree. She always avoided him – or perhaps toyed with him would be a better way to put it. The truth was that Kana Kó:re, in her heart, liked Ahentáken very much. She just was not sure how to act around boys her age. Even more, she felt a strange need to keep her emotions over the matter a secret.

Ahentáken, on the other hand, wore his heart on his

sleeve. His feelings toward Kana Kó:re were well known, especially to Kana Kó:re. There had never been any other girls in his eyes besides his bride to be. That was, of course, until he first laid eyes on Lucy, whom he knew as Tekawí:iaks. From the very beginning, the sight of the newcomer – the one the French called Marie – was too fascinating to ignore. It was not necessarily that Ahentáken was more attracted to her than he was to Kana Kó:re; he just found her so *interesting*. She was so completely outside the norm – and, try though he might, he could not shake the allure.

More and more, the boy had begun to show interest in Lucy, but the young lady really did not know what to make of it. On the one hand, she did not want to betray her new sister – especially considering the fact that Kana Kó:re did not seem to like her too much to begin with. But on the other hand, she could not help but be curious about Ahentáken, too. Not only was the Mohawk way of life new to her, the idea of spending time with boys was new and interesting, as well. What's more, something about Ahentáken – particularly whenever he was on horseback – reminded her of her forgotten life.

A day came when Lucy and Kawehnákens were tracking each other in the forest close to the village perimeter. This game was similar to the hiding game they played; only the hider was required to leave clues behind. Lucy was following the footsteps of her younger sister when she heard the crack of musket fire erupting from the village.

Startled, both Lucy and Kawehnákens darted away from their game and into the village. Hurrying to investigate, the two young girls saw a number of young men, including Ahentáken, practicing their shooting skills. Lucy's heart leapt as she saw the display. She had always felt a kind of affinity with the musket and, more than anything, wanted to grab up one of her own and join the boys.

Ahentáken had heard of Lucy's skill with a musket through the many stories that Young John had told about her initial journey to the village. As she approached, he smiled, feeling as though he had just read her mind. It was clear to him that Tekawí:iaks wanted to join in the practice. As she neared him, he held his musket by the barrel and presented it to her.

Lucy grinned broadly as she took the gun from Ahentáken's hands. Without even looking back at him, she turned to face the target in the distance – a small stick with a piece of leather attached near the top.

For some reason, Lucy could not bring herself to shoot. She was not quite sure what to do about the target since she had never seen one like it before. While she was sure that she was supposed to hit the leather, something about being in Ahentáken's presence made her want to second-guess everything she did. Doing something wrong, she felt, would have been a disaster. The embarrassment that she would surely feel would know no limits.

Lucy stood in the same position, holding the gun's barrel to her shoulder, level with her sight, for what seemed like a year. The boys had begun chuckling silently behind her, jabbing each other, smiling, and pointing at the scene jovially.

Just then, Kana Kó:re ceased what she was doing and noticed the group of boys. Particularly, she noticed Ahentáken's smiling uneasily at Tekawí:iaks as she steadied the site of the rifle on the target about fifty paces away. Kawehnákens seemed ready to tug on Tekawí:iaks' shirt-tail as the older sister readied herself to pull the trigger.

Kana Kó:re was stricken with the most powerful sense of jealousy that she had ever felt. A wave of anger washed over her as she hastily threw her weaving to the ground and stalked over towards the target. Just as she entered the line of Lucy's sight, Ahentáken quickly reached out his hand and swatted at the gun, causing Lucy to lower it to the ground.

"*Hold on, Tekawí:iaks,*" he said. "*Crazy girl wants to get herself killed.*"

"*Kana Kó:re,*" Kawehnákens called innocently, "*what are you doing? We're shooting here!*"

The boys all laughed, slapping each other on the shoulder and grinning at Kawehnákens. The little girl just blushed angrily and scowled back at the boys. She could not wait for the day that she would be big enough to hold a rifle of her own. Then, she would show the boys what real shooting looked like.

Everyone watched as Kana Kó:re pulled the target out of the ground and held it above her head. She smirked back at Lucy and then began walking in the opposite direction of the group. When she'd gone about 25 paces from the original spot of the target, she stopped and stuck the stick back into the ground.

When she was satisfied that the target was steady, she turned back to the group and yelled, "*If she is so good... let her shoot this!*"

The boys started laughing even harder than before. At that, Kana Kó:re began to laugh, as well, satisfied that she had made a fool out of her rival sister in front of her husband to be.

Lucy heard the laughter ringing in her ears. For some reason, it sparked a vision of townspeople dressed very similar to the Frenchmen she had seen earlier in the week. All of them were gathered around her, laughing at the way she was dressed.

"Little girls aren't supposed to wear leather breeches," one of the men said.

Lucy felt ashamed but somehow proud – as though the only thing she wanted more than to run away was to defy those who would laugh at her. From the moment she had pulled the trigger on the Huron, she knew that she was a good shot. In her recurring nightmares, too, she was almost always holding a musket. This target, even at its new distance, was not outside her range. She could hit it easily. The only question was, why wasn't she able to pull the trigger?

Kawehnákens tugged at Lucy's shirttail. *"Let's go,"* She said. *"Never mind this game, Tekawí:iaks. You can find me again."*

Lucy did not hear the little girl or notice the tugging. All at once, defiant anger had built up within her. She could not take the laughter any longer. Just then, she heard a loud explosion. When the smoke had cleared, the boys and Kana Kó:re's laughter had ceased.

Lucy looked down at the smoking musket in her hand, and then followed its line toward the target. The stick remained, but the patch of leather had been blown away.

Chapter Twelve

Driven

Maine Wilderness, October 1775

IT WAS THE END of October and the march north was beginning to toil on the Americans. Little did they know that their efforts were practically in vain. The dispatch that the Indian had carried had reached British hands mere days after Arnold's orders to march had gone out. With the dispatch came detailed plans of Arnold's intended invasion strategies. What they did not disclose was that Arnold had planned a two-pronged invasion, with Montgomery attacking Montreal.

Further complicating the matter was not just that Arnold had failed to account for the fact that almost every map used for battle plans on both the British and American fronts were distorted in order to throw off a potential enemy, but that he had selected the worst possible route. Not even the natives went that way. What he had thought to be 180 miles was actually quite a bit longer. The men knew it after weeks of marching – as they had already surpassed 180 miles and seemed no closer to their destination than when they'd started.

Captain Morgan seemed aloof during the several days that would follow – though every passing day burned him a little more inside. All around him, his men were suffering from starvation, malnutrition, and disease. As the march stretched the men past their point of endurance, desertion was also becoming a real problem.

Whenever Morgan brought his concerns up to Arnold, however, his request for quarter would always be turned down.

"The men can take it," Arnold would say, sitting high on his horse as he spoke. "Besides, we've only just begun. Think of the glory once we've arrived!"

"Sir, the men are starting to desert. We lose more each day," Captain Morgan would say.

"Cowards, the lot of them. The fates will deal with them as they may."

For what seemed like aloofness in Morgan almost appeared to be glee in Arnold. With each passing mile, he seemed to grow stronger and more delighted with himself.

"Keep faith, men," he would say. "We're nearly at the St. Lawrence. I can feel it! Can't you just smell the battle? The victory?"

By the two hundredth mile, what had once been an effective speech had lost its luster. More and more men were beginning to disbelieve the claim each time it was uttered. None of them realized it – as they did not have personal access to any maps, distorted or otherwise – but they had traversed the better part of Maine on foot in just over a week. Their progress was nothing short of miraculous, but it would be an effort poorly spent. None realized that they were marching to the most treacherous doom that they could possibly imagine.

"Victory is the only solution," Arnold yelled. "Victory is our only hope!"

That evening, Morgan and Arnold stood side by side, examining the map beneath their commanders' tent, just as they did every night.

"We're here, I'd say, Morgan," Arnold said, pointing to a spot on the map several dozen miles south of the St. Lawrence River. "That leaves only another few day's journey before we reach it. Then it's on to Quebec."

"I'll say again, sir, that we are losing dozens of men by the day," Morgan said. "The longer we march, the lesser our numbers."

"Not to worry, Morgan," Arnold said, placing his hand on his chest and straightening up proudly. "Numbers will not be a concern. The French will come to our aid."

"The Canadians? We've heard nothing from them. What makes you think they'll join us?"

Arnold ambled into the corner of the tent, facing away from Morgan, his hand still resting solemnly on his chest. Arnold looked upward, seeming to examine the top of the corner support pole as he spoke.

"Common enemy, you see," he said. "They'll join up when they see that they have a chance to finally drive the Brits out of their territory."

What Morgan did not realize was that, had the Canadians even been aware of the march through Maine, they would not have been in position to aid the Americans once they reached Quebec. In Canada, the militia was a French force controlled by an uneasy – or, more to the truth, untrusting – British government. In addition, their commanders publicly feared that the British would exact swift and total revenge, should the efforts against them fail. And since the Iroquois had made peace with the British, the last thing *Les Canadiens* needed was to square off with two military powers.

Will Ashley was cold and exhausted. Whatever beauty the New England autumn had once provided seemed dead to him. The rolling and constant palate of red, brown, orange, and yellow autumn leaves had lost their entire luster, and with each passing day, more of it seemed to turn to gray. Each hill that the marching army surmounted seemed like just one more hill too far. Will's legs had long since gone numb and his shoulders felt as though they would collapse at any moment under the weight of his heavy pack or boat.

Every step, by then, seemed to be its own little journey, as Will knew that any misstep, any stumble, would cause him to fall helplessly to the ground. And if he hit the ground, the young man was not sure if he'd ever be able to get up.

By then, word had gone round that more than three hundred men had deserted and turned back. When he'd first heard of deserters, Will had been angry, finding it hard to believe that a man would abandon something so significant simply because he was tired of walking. But these days, he could not help but identify with the notion. He wanted nothing more than to sink with a cup of tea in his hand into a deep wicker rocking chair on the front porch of his distant home. He daydreamed of Lucy. The mere thought of her brought him a hollow and pained feeling. Even if he were to desert, he realized, he'd been following the backs in front of him so blindly that he no longer knew where he was. Turning back may have proven to be the death of him.

I've got to press on, he told himself. *If I quit now, I've walked all this way for nothing. Plus, I'll be branded a traitor or deserter for the rest of my life – and I ain't neither.*

Will's friend David Weaver had contracted a fever that seemed to get worse with each passing day, and he was carried along on a makeshift litter. Their other friend Ben White had been asked to keep a close eye on David and report back to his commanding officer in the event that he took a turn for the worse. Each night, the news was progressively grimmer.

The thought of leaving David behind did not sit well with Will. He thought that if it were to happen, then all hope would be lost. The more Will thought about David's fate, the more he wanted to check up on his ailing friend, so the young soldier decided to slow his pace until the stretcher was at his side.

After what felt like an hour of falling behind, Will heard Ben's familiar call.

"Hey there, William!"

"Ben!" Will said. "How's the old faker doing back there?" Will looked down to see the pallid white face of his friend.

David opened his eyes and looked at Will. "Faker," he mumbled. "I'll show you faker."

"What?" Will asked, bringing his ear closer to his sick friend's mouth.

"Don't bother," Ben said. "He ain't been makin' much sense since 'bout three days ago."

"So he's not gettin' any better?"

"No...Fact, I'd say he's gotten worse. I'm just gonna run up to the front of the line to tell one of the officers."

Will looked hopelessly at David, who groaned deeply with a soft sort of rattling noise emitting from the back of his throat.

"This is it, W-W-Will," David said loudly. "I ain't gone make it."

Will felt a lump gather at the back of his throat. With it came a teary horizon on the edge of his eyes. He reached out and rubbed his friend's shoulder, wondering if the pain in his own legs and swollen feet would ever subside.

"Now don't you be sayin' things like that, Davy," Will said. "We're almost there. Then you can point and shoot your musket in whatever direction Morgan and Arnold tell you to."

David smiled weakly. He did not have the energy to hold even a smile any longer, much less a musket, and the brief glimpse of hope in his face melted quickly away. "Ain't gone make it, Will," he said again.

"Darn it, David," Ben said, apparently fed up with the fact that his friend was sick. "Dyin' now would be disobeyin' the captain's orders, you hear?"

"Yeah..." Will said. "Besides, we've lost too many good men already."

David reached up and grabbed Will's shoulder, whispering, "Don't be mad, but I was gonna turn back myself. Can ya imagine? Now where do you suppose that come from? I couldn't leave you fellas alone, though."

David then let out a sorrowful laugh that made Will want to laugh and cry at the same time.

At that moment, Will felt his fevered friend's hand slacken its grip against his shoulder and then go limp. "Davy!" Will said, noticing that his friend's eyes had gone hollow. "Davy!"

Ben joined in, returning from the front. "David?"

But David did not answer. Will eased his friend's hand

back on his chest and turned his face away from the body. One look at Will's eyes told Ben that David was dead. He had born the first hundred or so miles of marching and then the next few on a stretcher his friends had made for him, but in the end, the relentless fever proved too much for him. When the men finally took up camp for the evening – the boys arranged for a proper burial for their friend.

They placed David in the ground on the edge of a wide clearing beneath a small patch of willow trees already bare from the coming winter. One of the men in the company had been studying to become a minister before the outbreak of the revolution. His words over David's grave brought solace to the others while Will and Ben wept, no longer even trying their best to hide their emotions from the other men.

Over a month had passed since the troops had first set out from Newburyport. What little morale had remained was quickly beginning to wane.

Will and Ben spent what felt like the majority of that day hacking through the thick brush that lined this particular part of the northern wood. Periodically, Colonel Arnold would walk up and give encouragement to the men leading the party with their hacking blades.

"Not far now, men," he would say. "This brush should tell us that the river is just up ahead."

One of the older, grizzled soldiers turned to hand his blade back to Will, saying, "Your turn again, boy. Damn Arnold's been sayin' the big river's comin' up for miles now. Days."

Try though he might, not even Will could seem to get his spirits back up. The old man was right. Every hundred feet or so, the men would get to where they thought they had found a clearing – and a moment of hollow joy would erupt within them, spreading back through the pack like wildfire, only to be quashed just as quickly when no water appeared over the last bit of underbrush. Usually, it would be just another field, where they would set up and have a rest. However, now the rations were gone. There was nothing to forage, so there would be nothing to eat except boiled leather, tree bark, or whatever else could be found. At the end of each field would be more thick underbrush. And the hacking would begin anew.

It was time to rest. Will rested his head on his pack and fell into a deep sleep.

He could smell the smoke of campfire that was crackling before him, and Lucy was by his side.

"I remember many times back home after the evening meal," she said, just letting the words come. "I would see Father standing in front of the house – just looking off toward the wilderness. There were many times I wanted to run to him, but my mother always held me back. She'd tell me that he was communing with nature at those times, and it was my father's way of keeping in touch with his wandering spirit. Sometimes, I'd just watch my father, trying to imagine where he was in his mind's eye, and what he was doing. The strangest thing was that, after a while, it got to be as if I was there with him, somehow."

She stopped talking and looked at Will shyly. "Oh my, you must think me awful strange."

"Oh, no, Lucy. I don't think you're strange at all," Will said. "Fact is, it seems to me that women like you and your ma understand men like your pa and me."

Will noticed that Lucy was blushing as she looked intently into the fire, seeming to avoid the young man's gaze.

But Will continued, saying, "And I was thinkin' that

maybe someday, if I ever do settle down..." The young man's voice trailed off, as if he had lost his nerve to continue. Still, he could not take his eyes off Lucy.

—⁂—

"This ain't never gonna end, Will," Ben said the following morning when they were called to rise by the company's fife player.

Will rubbed the sleep out of his eyes. He did not reply, because there was nothing to say.

Just then, Arnold galloped by, waving his hands over his head wildly. "Rise up now, lads," he said. "The river's just ahead, just like I told you."

"Right," Ben said, grumbling.

Morgan strolled slowly behind the path that Arnold had taken. "He's right, men," he said. "Today, we carry the boats."

More grumbling erupted from the crowd of half-sleeping men.

"C'mon now, men," Morgan continued. "Not much farther. Six men to a boat."

Will finished massaging a little warmth back into his freezing toes, slipped his boots back on, and struggled to his feet. David followed suit, getting up gingerly as though he'd been carrying the weight of an entire continent on his back for many long weeks. Both boys reached back down and slowly slung their massive packs back on their backs before preparing themselves to meet up with a few other members of the company for boat detail. Together with four others, they would carry an additional load on this day. With any luck, Arnold's story about "just a few more miles" would not be a lie this time.

Chapter Thirteen

Tuck

Mohawk Valley, November 1775

THE SNOW WOULD BE falling soon. The sky seemed to stand still, a band of unmoving clouds on the horizon frozen in place by the growing cold. Not even the browning grass seemed capable of waving in the barely perceptible breeze. The trees had been laid bare, all of them seeming to brace for the heavy loads that they would soon carry during the snowy season.

This was the time of year that all the remaining hunters and trappers in the region headed home – either to warmer climates or to latch themselves in for the winter. As the most logical path to the south led wagon trains and horse parties very near Young John's village, more often than not, the travelers would pass through and pay the Mohawks a visit in the hopes of picking up items and useful tidbits necessary for survival during the harsh journey that lie ahead. Young John was a particular fan of this time of year because the desperation in the eyes of the whites often led to good bartering situations for the intrepid Mohawk.

By this point, Lucy had been with her new tribal family for several months. More and more, she was beginning to feel like a part of the clan. And the feeling was certainly reciprocated – particularly by Young John, who did all that he could to make sure that his adopted daughter was accepted and included in everything that the family did. Lucy was beginning to love Young John like a father, which was a good and natural thing since he was the only father figure she could recall.

That morning, Kawehnákens waked Lucy hurriedly. The little girl wore a short and simple dress made of buckskin. Her arms and legs were covered with leathery braces of animal fur designed to keep her extremities warm. Earlier in the week, her jet-black hair had been braided here and there by mother Konwáhne and Kana Kó:re – a style that she still wore on this morning. Lucy could recall the pride that her youngest sister seemed to project as her mother and eldest sister fawned over her hair. Not really one for such girly fare, Lucy had kept to herself during the braiding, mostly just laughing at the delighted look on her little sister's face.

"Hurry, Tekawí:iaks," Kawehnákens said as she shook Lucy awake.

"What is it?" Lucy asked, sleepily rising to a sitting position.

Lucy could hear people moving excitedly about outside the house. As she approached the entrance, she could make out the sounds of pots and pans clanking and clunking.

The early morning sky was now fully gray, signaling that there would be rain and maybe even snow that day. Joseph Tucker had come to call, bringing all of his wares strapped to the backs of five gray mules and led by a large black horse pulling a small cart. The train of animals was certainly impressive for one man to handle, but definitely made for a pretty comical sight as it awkwardly approached. Tucker would lean forward in his saddle and stroke his horse's mane. Then, whenever he felt a tug on the line connecting him to his mules, he would turn around and bark commands at the offending animal that had fallen behind.

Joe Tucker was a small black man in his 60's. His narrow shoulders and barrel chest made him look a little top-heavy as he sat low in his saddle.

Tucker had spent most of his adult life trapping, selling, and trading with Indians from all tribes and clans. His travels took him from Massachusetts to the great Champlain annually. As any Iroquois elder would have told Lucy, had she asked, Tucker was a great pleasure to do business with. He was always fair and never carried any assumptions about his buyers. Unlike many of the whites who came to the area, Tucker did not seem to be out to swindle anybody. More than anything, he just appeared to enjoy his chosen lifestyle – and that joy carried over to every bartered transaction.

Once he reached the edge of the village, the strange but endearing man pulled his horse to a halt and walked spryly into the compound. His horse and mules, he pulled in tow.

Over the years, Tucker had earned the trust of the tribe so he was allowed to walk unimpeded into the heart of the village. Regardless of the conditions of the day, he stood behind his merchandise and his word. This day, it seemed, was no different, as Tucker stood proudly in the center of the village and called out to anyone who would listen.

Several women gathered around him and his horse. Some began plucking at Tucker's many wares. He tried to address each of them individually, smiling proudly as they examined his items. Now and then, he would hold up a few fingers and the villagers would counter by holding up fewer fingers. Usually, he would just laugh and nod his head politely.

Having nothing to trade, Lucy simply stopped and stared at Tucker. His high, prominent forehead was flanked on either side by wooly, graying hair. His nose was large and flat and he had just about the kindliest brown eyes that Lucy had ever seen. But his most predominant feature was his thick, heavy eyebrows.

The young lady could place it, but there was something familiar about Tucker. She was certain that she had never seen him before, and yet something about him made her feel a little dizzy.

Who is this man, she thought. *He leads his string of mules as if they were on parade.* She laughed as Tucker sashayed back from his horse to deal with a woman who was checking a large metal cooking pot hanging from the flank of his lead mule.

Kawehnákens laughed, too. In fact, the little girl was giggling more and more as the two sisters drew nearer the whole scene. She seemed excited, as if she were on her way to meet with an old friend. Lucy chuckled as Kawehnákens picked up a pine twig and snapped it in half. The little girl then placed the two pieces up to her eyebrows and danced around Lucy, making fun of the old man.

Kawehnákens danced with her eyes closed and laughed, saying, *"Look, Tekawí:iaks, I have caterpillar eyes!"*

But before Kawehnákens knew it, she was brushing up against the old trader, who understood enough Mohawk to know he was being teased.

"Caterpillars?" he said. "Careful, little girl! If those turn into butterflies, you'll get flown away!"

Tuck had known the little girl since her birth and always had a wonderful time with her. They were almost constantly teasing each other. At that moment, he seemed to be reveling in Kawehnákens' infectious laughter.

"Would you look at this, Billy," Tucker said loudly, smiling and still staring down at the little Mohawk. "'Another day of rain ahead for us, my son, and all this silly girl can think about is dancin'.'"

Lucy and Kawehnákens stood silently.

"Who is he speaking with?" Lucy whispered to her sister.

"His horse," Kawehnákens responded with a giggle. Others standing nearby also began to chuckle.

"He speaks with his horse?"

"Yep," Tucker responded as he passed. He tugged on the brim of his hat in greeting to Lucy. "And he speaks with me," he said as his big brow came down heavy with a wink.

Lucy was a little taken aback and confused by his strange response, but as the other people began to laugh, she did as well.

The girls backed off slightly as several men from the village approached with armfuls of furs. Young John's pelts were always the high point of the bartering. He was widely regarded as one of the greatest hunters in the entire region.

Without a word, the men dropped their pelts into piles on the frigid, dusty ground and walked straight up to the mules, rifling through Tucker's wares along with the villagers who had already picked things over. Several of these men began pulling down the items that they were interested in. Like many of the villagers, Young John had his eye on some iron skillets and scalding pots. He reached for the items, pulled them down off the mule, and placed them on the ground at his feet. He then looked Tuck square in the eyes.

Lucy watched in awe as Tuck held up ten fingers. Young John shook his head back and forth and held up five. The black man then made a funny look that blended into a knowing little half-smile. He held up seven fingers. Lucy looked quickly at her adoptive father and watched as the proud Mohawk nodded his head solemnly. The deal had been made for seven pelts. As Young John shuffled back to gather his furs, others followed his lead and the process was repeated over and over.

Later that morning, Wilkes and his party dressed, as colonials with British trappings to show that they were loyalists, lead their horses slowly into a Mohawk Village. They hoped to enlist the services of a few guides to assist them in locating the outlaw Lucy Killgrew. As they made there way to the village center, Kawehnákens darted out from seemingly nowhere. Wilkes' horse bolted slightly, causing him to lose his grip on the reins. Hamilton quickly settled the horse down and handed the animal back to his commander. He stared menacingly at the little girl, but she was quickly forgotten when his attention was drawn to her older sister yelling her name.

"Kawehnákens, I have told you many times to stay with me. Father will be angry if I tell him."

Lucy was about to continue her chastisement of the little girl when she noticed the men standing before her.

Wilkes instantly recognized her and was amazed that

she did not yell out her recognition of him.

Lucy thought there was something familiar about him, but just like everything else, the feeling was without substance. She took Kawehnákens by the hand and led her away. After putting a little distance between herself and the men, she looked back and was immediately drawn to Wilkes' cold stare. She continued to move on until she was out of his sight.

Wilkes leaned over to Hamilton and whispered, "It's her! What I don't understand is why didn't she cry out, and what is she doing in this God-forsaken place?"

"Maybe it's not her. After all, she was speaking their gibberish," replied Hamilton.

"No, it's her. I'll never forget that one," said Wilkes.

"Perhaps she's lost her memory," suggested Hamilton. "I've heard that people go into a state of shock after Indian attacks. If she is not calling out it for help, it is probably because of that very reason."

"It matters not," Wilkes responded. "We'll make camp outside the village and bide our time."

"Sir," said Hamilton, "what makes you believe these Indians will give her over to us?"

"Hamilton, my dear, dear fellow," Wilkes said coldly, "I don't intend on seeking their permission."

About an hour into a counting game that she was playing with Kawehnákens, Lucy was feeling a little bored. Therefore, she told her young sister that she felt like taking a walk. To her surprise, her little sister did not seem to want to join her. Kawehnákens did look tired, so Lucy figured she planned to take a nap – which was very unusual for this high-energy little girl. Either way, Lucy did not argue. She had few chances to be alone and rather enjoyed them. Furthermore, on this day, she was far too curious about Tucker to allow him to go uninvestigated any longer.

As she softly approached the edge of the village, Lucy noticed Tucker feeding his animals. Her curiosity getting the better of her, she walked straight up to him. "Your horse's name is Billy?" she asked. It felt strange to be speaking English again. She had not done it in so long.

Tucker jumped, startled. He obviously had not noticed Lucy's approach. "Well," Tucker responded, "there I go forgettin' my manners. Name's Tucker. Joe Tucker. But you can call me Tuck." He smiled.

"Tuck," Lucy said, shaping the words as though they meant something a little deeper to her than just a strange man's name.

"Sure," Tucker said cheerfully. "Everyone else calls me that, 'ceptin' the Frenchies. They call me Tuck-air." The old man allowed the last syllable to carry a little in a higher pitch.

Lucy laughed, recognizing that Tucker was making fun of the French accent.

"Course, ya'll ready know Billy, I reckon," Tuck continued.

Lucy nodded abruptly. The old man seemed harmless enough. Lucy hesitated for a moment, shifting a little in place. Finally, she said, "Hello, Tuck. My name's Tekawí:iaks. The French call me Marie."

Tucker looked at Lucy, his large eyebrows reaching their highest arch. He appeared to be a little puzzled. "I ain't seen you here before," he said. "Where you come from?"

"In truth, I'm not sure," Lucy said with a shrug. "I don't remember anything before Young John."

"You're foolin'."

"No ...no, I've been trying really hard, too. But nothing

is clear in my head."

Lucy gazed deep within Tucker's eyes. "Joshua," she said distantly.

"Who's Joshua?" Tuck asked, working to adjust the bit in Billy's mouth.

Lucy looked at the old man, puzzled, and continued to focus only on his eyes.

Suddenly, she was transferred to a different place, as if riding the back of a walking dream. "What's your name?" she asked as she stood and began to draw a bucket of water from a well.

"My name's Joshua," the old black man said. "The Redcoats told me I was free. But Mr. Black never owned me. He was jus' my friend."

Lucy pulled a metal dipper from a peg on the side of the well and dipped it into the bucket.

"Mr. Black made me a free man. He taught me his trade," Joshua said as Lucy again knelt down by his side.

The black man's shirt was covered with blood, but it was hard for Lucy to tell whether it was his or Mr. Black's.

She set her pistol on the ground and lifted the cup of water to Joshua's lips.

"Drink this, and then we'll see how badly you're hurt," she said as Joshua began to drink slowly from the cup.

"Joshua...Mr. Black? I don't know what yer sayin', girl," Tucker said loudly as he softly shook Lucy's shoulder.

Lucy's concentration was broken. She quickly turned her head away from Tucker, feeling both embarrassed and frustrated by what had just happened. After a moment, she looked back at Billy his horse solemnly and said, "It's good to meet you too, Billy."

Tuck stood and smiled his approval, though he still looked a little confused by what he had just witnessed. "Well, young miss," he said, "snow will be here soon. And these people allow me to have a little cabin not too far from here. Nice people, them Mohawks. It's where I winters. I leave in the spring."

"Oh," Lucy said distantly, wishing she had something a little more interesting to add to the conversation.

"I'll need to be goin' now," Tuck continued. "But I'll ask round 'bout you when I gets a chance."

Lucy nodded silently as she looked at the ground beneath her feet.

"But for now, you're with good people," Tuck said reassuringly. "Strange people, though. Why, I seen them take on colonists and Frenchies, leavin' nobody." Tuck shook his head as he spoke. "An' think nothin' on it." He then placed his hands in his pockets and looked proudly at the pretty young lady standing awkwardly before him. "Here you are a livin' with the Bears."

Lucy knew that the strange man was referring to the Bear Clan. She smiled, blushing a little.

"A great an' terrible land," Tuck said as he turned and pulled his team of horses away. After a few steps, he turned and looked back over his shoulder. "I'll check in on you in the spring 'fore I head out again."

"Maybe I should leave in the spring, too," Lucy said, startled by her forward suggestion.

The old man looked at Lucy and a sense of sadness seemed to cross behind his eyes. He turned back to Lucy and stood directly in front of her again. Grasping her shoulders gently, he spun her around to face the forest that surrounded the village. "Young lady, look as far as you can see and tell me what's out there."

"Trees," Lucy replied.

"That's right, child," Tuck said. "Trees. It's all trees. An' it be all the same here too. Here…there…and all over."

"I don't understand."

"Listen to me, child," he said seriously. "What I'm sayin' is that if it ain't here, you sure ain't gonna find it out there. At least, not now." Tuck shook his head slowly and a bit sadly.

Lucy did not speak. Though her heart was filled with anguish, she could not help but admit to herself that the old man was probably right. If she did head out on her own, how could she find what she was looking for if she did not know what it was?

"I ain't never said this to anyone before, and I don't know why I'm tellin' you," Tuck said suddenly. The old man stepped back, looking as though he was thinking deeply for the moment. "I had me a daughter once … long time ago."

Lucy thought she could see tears forming at each corner of Tuck's deep brown eyes.

"I was out in the fields southways from here," the old man continued. "And when I come back, she was gone." Tuck turned his head completely away from Lucy. "The man who owned me sold her and I ain't never seen her again. I tried to find her, but it weren't no use."

Lucy felt herself begin to tear up, too. It was a strange feeling. She had not felt like crying about anything but her lost past for a very long time. She opened her mouth to speak, but no words came out.

"You go out there now or in the spring," Tucker said as he looked off into the forest, "land keeps goin', and you just might never come back."

Lucy nodded.

"Don't worry, child. When you remember, you'll know just what to do."

Lucy took great comfort in those words. Lately, she had begun to lose much of her hope that she would ever know her true history. That part of her that seemed dead was revived almost instantly by a few kind words from a strange man whom she had never met but longed to know.

"Meanwise, stay with the Bears," Tuck said, abruptly turning back to grab Billy's reins. "Learn from them – grow strong with them. Do that, child, an you'll never lose your way."

Chapter Fourteen

Kawehnákens

THE MOHAWK WOULD WAKE at different times, depending on the season. The sun served as the only indication that it was time to rise. Now that the ground was cold and the sunrise came later, the Mohawk's day started a little later, too.

On one such morning, before the sun had come up, the sound of young boys running and laughing opposite the wall behind the head of her bed abruptly awoke Kawehnákens. The little girl rubbed her eyes and sat up, looking around. Just as suddenly as the sounds awoke her, the commotion seemed to disappear. Strain though she might to discover the source of the noise, everyone was clearly still asleep.

After a few moments of silent sitting, Kawehnákens

looked over at Lucy, who was thrashing violently from side to side, obviously reliving the torment of her recurring nightmare.

Having learned of the consequences of waking her sister in the middle of one of these dreams – mostly confused yelling and terrified sweating on the part of the older girl – Kawehnákens decided to ignore her and walk to the entrance of her home.

Once she stepped into the pale morning light, to her delight, she saw the shadows of several adolescent boys running past another shelter, chasing what looked like a young deer that had wandered into the compound. The boys had managed to coordinate their efforts and now silently funneled the deer down the main road of the village and into the surrounding fields. Several of them held bows.

Kawehnákens trotted out to follow as the boys ran into the field in pursuit of the fawn. The boys proved to be far too fast for her, though. She fell behind, slowing to a light jog as she watched the boys dart into the trees lining the edge of the field.

Undaunted, she trotted purposefully up to the perimeter of the forest. The darkness within seemed overwhelming; the thick branches, despite their lack of leaves, provided a canopy that shielded the forest floor from the majority of the ample moonlight. Kawehnákens hesitated. Just as she was considering turning back, a slight, shadowy movement in the distance caught her attention.

By that point, the boys were nowhere to be found, but the movement was still intriguing. *Maybe I can scare out my own deer,* she thought hopefully. *Maybe it will be a buck!* Suddenly, she wished she had brought her little bow with her. The girl was too young to realize that the tiny bow would not come close to piercing a deer's hide.

However, she always felt like a celebrated warrior whenever she held it. *Just like father,* she often thought.

Drawn by her intense curiosity, Kawehnákens moved in past the first line of trees and caught another faint glimpse of something moving in the distance. Thinking that she had, indeed, stumbled across a deer of her own, she put her hand to her mouth to restrain a giggle as she drew nearer the source of the movement.

She proceeded silently, careful to feel the ground first with her feet before stepping down with her full weight – just as her father had taught her. Whether the girl had taken quickly to the lesson or whether her slight weight contributed to her ability to keep silent, Young John had never been quite sure. Still, he had always been so proud of his youngest daughter's abilities to move undetected. Now, if only she could keep from laughing while she did...

To her credit, on this occasion, Kawehnákens had managed to stave off her laughter long enough to reach a clearing that surrounded her quarry. As she reached the edge of an evergreen shrub that separated her from the clearing, she peered into the expanse before her. What she saw almost startled her out of her wits.

When she realized that she had come across a group of four white men, she dropped low behind a row of small pines.

"This makes no sense, Mr. Wilkes," said Hamilton.

"What do you mean, Hamilton?" Wilkes replied.

In the brush, Kawehnákens stifled a growing urge to cough. She had heard of the cruelty of the whites. She knew very well that getting caught would be the worst possible thing that she could do.

"Well, sir," Hamilton continued, "I don't know why we just don't go into the village and demand that they hand the girl over to us."

"Why, Hamilton, you surprise me," Wilkes said cheerfully. "You presuppose that we intend to bring the girl in for punishment."

Kawehnákens leaned out carefully from behind her tree. She watched as Hamilton looked at Wilkes incredulously.

"You mean we're not?" he said.

"Again, you surprise me," Wilkes said, absently digging in the soil with a long stick. "Bringing prisoners back would only reopen the issue. Do you honestly think that I would have the matter of the escapes of this girl and the others brought up again? No, Hamilton, she'll meet her fate at the hands of these savage Indians. At least that's what my report will say."

The young girl, her excitement getting the best of her, could sit still no longer. She needed a closer look. Bracing herself on the base of the pine, she rose slowly to her feet and crept from the trunk of one small tree to the next, trying desperately not to make a sound.

Muffled sounds once again reverberated in Lucy's head. The familiar yet strange man approached her as always. On this occasion, Lucy sat under a tree, writing in a small book, when she sensed another presence. Startled, she looked around, but realized with horror that her vision blurred.

She heard a twig snap.

Wilkes took a deep breath to regale Hamilton further when he heard the distinct sound of a snapping twig. He turned in the direction of the sound, his eyes settling on the row of small pines at the edge of the clearing.

Wilkes looked back to see if the others had noticed. Hamilton, at least, certainly had. He sat wide-eyed, waiting for a signal from his superior officer. Wilkes obliged, waving his hand in the direction of the sound and then placing his index finger to his lips, motioning for silence.

The men rose and walked cautiously in the direction of the sound.

─❦─

Despite the distance of her memory, Lucy was keenly aware that she had just hidden something. Reaching back with her hand, she felt beneath a root of the tree against which she was sitting. Her fingertips grazed across what felt like a leather-bound book.

Satisfied that her secret was safe beneath the tree, she rose to her feet in hopes of investigating the sound that she had just heard.

Suddenly, a hand came from behind and clamped over her mouth. Lucy closed her eyes tightly as she felt herself flung against the trunk of the tree.

In the distance of her mind, she could hear a faint scream. It was youthful and subtle – familiar yet somehow unfamiliar, like the voice of a person whose laughter she had heard many times, but still could not place. The sound did not come from her own throat. Instead, the cry came from someone else … someone in danger.

Lucy woke with a start from her nightmare. Instinctively, she darted her eyes in the direction of her younger sister's bed. She noticed immediately that Kawehnákens was gone.

─❦─

Hearing the sound of the twig that she had just broken, the little girl moved swiftly in the early morning darkness, her arms brushing softly against the reaching, scratchy hands of pine tree branches. Her head moving quickly from side to side in search of a suitable hiding place, Kawehnákens settled on a spot between a stand of trees and quickly disappeared within them.

When he reached the point where he had last seen the young girl, Wilkes slowed his pace – motioning for the others, who were stalking about twenty paces behind, to do the same. An expert tracker himself, Wilkes was practically fuming that again he had allowed a girl to slip from sight. He looked around wildly, and then hurriedly returned to his anxious men.

"She's gone," he said, his eyes darting nervously. "She'll be warning the others soon, so best get ready." He primed his musket, dropping a length of powder into the barrel and sifting through his sack of pellets.

The others followed suit with no words spoken between them. Any reasonable British soldier knew that if the Mohawks were alerted to their presence, it was only a matter of time before they were discovered. Being discovered under these circumstances would not be a good thing either – as the Mohawks would likely interpret the uninvited presence of the British as an intrusion on their territory.

Upon finishing with his musket, Wilkes crouched low, trying to think of his next move. Little did he know that Kawehnákens had not returned to the village, as any sensible young warrior would have. Thus, he did not know that the villagers had no knowledge of his presence. Furthermore, he was unaware that the Mohawk he had followed was actually a four-year-old girl.

Meanwhile, Kawehnákens remained hidden in a small groove under a large tree that had fallen many years ago. The tree's ancient trunk bent awkwardly and jaggedly from the frosty soil beneath its roots to the jagged rocks of the ditch wall that now held its trunk in place. Kawehnákens found herself thanking the tree for providing a safe haven on this chilly and frightful morning.

Although she was indeed well concealed, Kawehnákens knew that she would not be able to remain in such a confining space indefinitely. Despite the gravity of the situation, she could not help but recall her hiding games with Tekawí:iaks. More than anything, she just hoped that, like the game, someone would come to find her soon – and she preferred that that someone not be a white man.

Camped in the modest cabin just outside the village, Tuck had been startled from sleep by the sound of the Mohawk boys chasing a fawn into the brush. Ever the curious one, he could not help but pull his boots and jacket on and head out to investigate.

Figuring that he had nothing to fear from Mohawk man or boy, he stumbled awkwardly into the forest, hoping to catch a glimpse of an Indian hunt in action. He had heard that they hunted methodically, in utter silence and with deadly precision.

He waved his arms before him, clearing branches out of his way as he stomped through the underbrush, second-guessing himself as to whether it had been a good idea to venture out into the cold in the first place.

As Wilkes crouched down, he heard the unmistakable sound of someone coming toward him. The sound was actually reassuring, because he knew that no worthwhile Indian warrior would approach without the cover of stealth. He knew that if his attacker were Mohawk, he would not have heard anything until it was too late. However, this person or animal was clearly making no effort to conceal its hasty and frantic movements.

Wilkes turned and watched as a short black man staggered into view. He was not sure if the man's eyes had not yet adjusted to the darkened landscape or if he was just too blind to see him, but it was not until Wilkes was within feet of the old man that he was actually noticed.

"Well, hello, sir," the black man said loudly. "Wait a minute…you ain't supposed to—"

Fitzwater jacked Tuck in the face with the butt of his musket. The other private, Harris, followed suit, and Wilkes reveled in the opportunity silently to beat the black man into submission.

It did not take long before Tuck was completely subdued.

Lucy, her eyes still adjusting to the darkness, moved through the house and noticed that Kana Kó:re was gone, too. At that moment, a wave of relief washed over her as she assumed that Kawehnákens had simply gone exploring with her older sister.

Lucy quietly stepped around the clutter in the center of the room and strolled into the dawning sky. Still early as it was, a stark chill lingered in the air from the night. After rubbing her palms together, Lucy held her hands over the ashy embers that remained in the fire pit. Dissatisfied with the warmth, she decided to start a new fire. She grabbed some kindling from a wooden box and a short stick from near the pit. Placing the kindling into the pit, she struck two pieces of flint over the kindling, just as Konwáhne had taught her. Since many of the embers were still glowing from the previous night's fire, Lucy's kindling was soon ablaze. She turned quickly to grab a stumpy log from the pile next to the house and dropped it carefully into the small flame. To her delight, the log caught and the fire grew rapidly.

Smiling, she stood up, telling herself that it would be

nice to sit by the fire with a blanket from inside. Just as she was about to walk back into her shelter, Kana Kó:re approached from around the corner.

"Where's Kawehnákens?" Lucy asked when she noticed that Kana Kó:re was alone.

"I have not seen her," Kana Kó:re replied coldly. *"Is she not in the house?"* Then, the young lady stiffened. *"Is she not in the house?"* she asked again, louder this time.

"No," Lucy said quickly, the concern growing within her. *"Quick! We must find where she is."*

The two girls darted away from the house and split up, combing the village for any sign of Kawehnákens. Each progressed from one end of the village to the other, checking every corner and looking behind every pile of pelts or wood.

As Lucy searched, a growing dread began to well up inside her. It was not like her little sister to be away alone – much less without someone knowing where she was. For all her free-spirited faults, Kawehnákens had always been careful to let her elders know where they could find her.

As the daylight grew, several other villagers crept out of their homes and began stretching their limbs. Several of them noticed the frantic search that the girls were performing. Curious, they joined in the search.

Despite their efforts, Kawehnákens was nowhere to be found.

Lucy met Kana Kó:re once again in front of their house. The look of dread on both girls' faces spoke volumes about the desperation of the situation.

"We must tell Father," Kana Kó:re said, trembling.

Chapter Fifteen

A Matter of Fate

LUCY AND KANA KÓ:RE followed their father Young John, as they and three other men from the village fanned out along the forest perimeter. As they drew nearer to the tree line, Lucy noticed a familiar footprint among the many others. It was small, rounded, and barely perceptible in the frosty dirt. Lucy had played the hiding game long enough with her younger sister to know that this track belonged to Kawehnákens.

With a start, she realized something: She and Kawehnákens had never been anywhere near this area before. If her sister had ventured this far from the village, something must have drawn her there.

"Father," Lucy called softly over her shoulder, *"I've found a track."*

Young John fell in line behind his daughter and followed her lead into the woods. Lucy swept her eyes rapidly across the ground as she swiftly made her way deeper into the forest. Her skin crawled with nervous anticipation and her muscles grew tense, urging her onward despite her mounting worry.

Young John understood his new daughter enough to know that she was on to something. *Good at whatever she puts her mind to,* he thought as he panted shallowly, following Lucy through the trees and shrubs without a sound.

As Tuck returned to consciousness, the old man could swear that he heard the sound of approaching footsteps. From a kind of stir in the air, he knew very well that it meant the Mohawk were on the hunt. On this day, looking with disgust at the British men who had beaten him, he could guess their prey. He smiled inwardly as he imagined the vindication that would shortly come.

Tuck watched as Wilkes, Hamilton, and Harris stiffened, listening intently. Fitzwater was still standing ominously over the black man, not seeming to sense the approaching doom as he poised the butt of his musket over his captive's face.

Meanwhile, Tuck noticed that Wilkes, Harris, and Hamilton had crouched down and were readying their muskets on their shoulders. He then turned his attention to the other end of the clearing, maybe ten feet away, where he realized in horror that his young friend Kawehnákens was gagged and bound to a large oak tree at the bottom of a gently sloping gully. Next to her was the mouth of a jagged crevice that looked to extend down at least forty feet before opening up to the valley below.

"Stand down, man," Wilkes whispered in the Fitzwater's direction. "And ready yourself for the assault."

Doing what he was told, Fitzwater left Tuck's side and fell in line with the other three, crouching down on one knee and bringing the butt of his musket to the flat of his shoulder.

Twenty meters away, Young John picked up the distinctive clicking sound of a musket's hammer as it is drawn back. He reached out to grab his daughters and pull them to a halt, but Lucy and Kana Kó:re heard it, too, and stopped before he could even touch them. At that moment, Young John was thankful that he had been so thorough in training his young daughters in the ways of the warrior. Most fathers in the village trained their women to fight only in the event that the village was attacked – but Young John knew that a time would come when every man, woman, and child would need to go on the offensive. Therefore, he taught his eldest daughters how to stalk an enemy and his youngest daughter how to evade one. He did not know how important those lessons would prove to be on this fateful day.

Lucy and Kana Kó:re both knew that to alert their enemies to their presence would cause those who had them targeted to open fire. Until they knew from which direction the men would shoot – to say nothing of just how many men there were – it did not make sense to charge or even call out an alert to the others.

Young John looked over his shoulder and saw the other three members of his clan creeping forward from beyond the underbrush. They had apparently noticed Young John and his daughters crouching in silence and had taken that as a cue to approach with caution.

Young John turned to face the approaching warriors and motioned in the direction in front of him with his head.

As any Mohawk knew, this was the signal to surround the location and spring an attack from all sides.

As his men prowled into place, Young John stepped over to his daughters and placed a hand on each girl's shoulder. He gently pressed downward, causing the girls to crouch down further and then lie prone on their stomachs.

Lucy turned her head, meaning to protest – she knew she could handle herself in battle, after all – but then thought better of it and remained still. Making any noise would surely spoil the entire effort.

Once he had successfully managed to ease his daughters to the ground and out of harm's way, Young John skulked to the edge of the brush, within feet of the waiting British soldiers, who faced in a direction perpendicular to their attacker. The proud Mohawk was so close that he could have reached out and grabbed Harris' earlobe as the soldier crouched beside him. Despite their close proximity, the men did not notice the Mohawks watching over them. Young John used the opportunity to scan the area for his daughter. His eyes fell upon Tuck, who had propped himself up on his elbows. Blood flowed from the old man's nose and down to his white undershirt. His jacket was flung open and hung off his shoulders, which were badly stained with blood, as well.

At that moment, Young John noticed a familiar face appearing from behind the shrubs on the opposite side of the clearing. It was a member of his attack party. He had found his place and was signaling to Young John that he was ready to spring the attack.

Young John returned the signal with one of his own: Hold. He still needed to locate his daughter. As he scanned along the line of shrubs, he noticed several other faces come into view. All three of the other members of his attack party were now accounted for – and they were all in place, awaiting his battle cry.

Then, as Young John's gaze reached the far end of the clearing, his heart skipped a beat. The land bent down into a gully that was bisected by a large oak tree. Despite the dip in the ground, Young John could make out the top of his daughter's head. Her dark, braided hair was barely visible above the crest of the hill. After a few seconds of watching Kawehnákens' head bob around aimlessly, Young John was granted a view of his daughter's face as she rolled her head back and looked at the sky. Her mouth was gagged, muffling her screams and her strained movements suggested that she was bound to the tree behind her.

At that moment, one of the soldiers whispered loudly, "Sir, what of the girl?"

"Quiet, Hamilton," Wilkes replied through his teeth. "We may not be alone."

Young John eased back into the underbrush just as Wilkes' eyes passed by the spot where he was standing. Judging from the lack of movement from within the clearing, Young John knew that he had not been detected.

"Let the girl go," Tuck yelled from behind the men.

"Shut him up!" Wilkes barked.

"With pleasure," Fitzwater said, getting up and whacking Tuck across the face with the butt of his gun.

"And, Hamilton," Wilkes said, "get rid of the girl. Toss the child down the crevice. She's no concern of mine."

For all the brutality issued by Wilkes and for the many times Hamilton had stood in silent witness to his wicked temperament, the Corporal's conscience could resist no longer. His anger surged to the surface and boiled over like water in a pot as he stated defiantly, "I will not, sir!"

If no one else could see it, Hamilton could. As far as he was concerned, evil men and hostiles surrounded him. He was a gentleman and he would go out as such if need be.

"Upon mine honor," said Wilkes. "This is hardly the time to break ranks."

"Upon your honor? Sir, you have no honor if you harm this child." He replied, walking to the girl and taking her under his protection.

The two privates could not believe that the corporal dare to mutiny. Fitzwater moved toward Hamilton but hesitated when the corporal directed his musket toward Wilkes.

"I knew it would come to this. You are indeed an untrustworthy fellow. You're finished, you know," said Wilkes in a whispered, scolding tone.

Lucy winced, knowing that she was the only one near the scene who could understand the words. She desperately wanted to call out and warn her father, but she knew that doing so could lead to the death of the entire attack party. There were only four Mohawks, after all – and they were badly under-armed – and she had heard the voices of at least three soldiers who were presumably carrying weapons. Something about one of the voices gave Lucy pause, however. At first the voice had only a distant familiarity to it, but the moment she heard the words, "She's no concern of mine," the crack of thunder echoed in her mind. For some unknown reason, hearing this voice brought great anger to her heart.

Lucy picked her head up to see that her father was crouched with his back to the underbrush that separated him from the clearing. He was soundlessly drawing an arrow out of his quiver and prepping his bow. The girl knew that her father could not possibly see what the whites were doing.

Hamilton had untied Kawehnákens and taken the child up in his arms. As he moved farther away from the group, he pulled the gag out of the little girl's mouth just before tripping over a branch in the dark. He cried out as he tumbled over the embankment into the crevice.

Lucy heard the unmistakable thud of a blunt object meeting heavily with flesh and then the scream of her youngest sister as she fell clutching tightly to Hamilton.

At the sound of the scream, Young John let out a wail of his own – his was a call to battle for the surrounding attack party. The timing of the call was off, however, as it would have been beneficial for Young John to wait for all of the soldiers to fall back into line again. As it was, four Mohawks charged in to attack three scattered British soldiers with muskets fully loaded.

During the charge, two of the Mohawks were killed, one by Harris' pistol and the other by Wilkes' musket. Young John lunged toward Wilkes, who was crouched nearest his angle of attack. At that moment, Wilkes rose up and met Young John's powerful charge with his shoulder. The two men stumbled backward in opposite directions, Wilkes drawing a knife from out of his boot and Young John reaching for the hatchet slung over his back.

The fourth and only other remaining member of the Mohawk attack party wrestled with Fitzwater, who still had not fired his gun.

Below in the crevice Hamilton gasped in pain, trying to turn toward the young girl. She lay silent, looking deeply into his eyes. "I'm so sorry," he whispered before expiring.

The sound of the gunfire caused the entire Mohawk village to spring into action. All the men and older boys grabbed their bows and rifles and charged into the forest.

Wilkes managed to stave off the attack from Young John, actually wounding the arm of the proud warrior.

He reached for the pistol at his side as the Indian stumbled back into the underbrush. At that moment, the only remaining uninjured Mohawk sprang off Harris – whom he had just dispatched with the blade of his tomahawk – and tackled Wilkes. As he did so, Fitzwater fired, striking the Indian square in the back, killing him instantly.

His strength redoubled, Young John leapt back into the fray, charging Fitzwater with his hatchet extended above his head. The Mohawk proved too swift for the soldier, and Young John toppled him to the ground.

Lucy, having taken all the waiting quietly that she could muster, crawled into the clearing undetected. She snaked her way around Tuck's head and up to the body of the dead private. Without making a sound, she grabbed the still-loaded musket that the soldier had been carrying.

As Young John drew his arm back to bring down a killing stroke on Fitzwater, Wilkes reared up on his knees and drew his hammerlock pistol. However, before he could fire on the Mohawk, Lucy sprang to her feet and shot, striking Wilkes in the thigh and causing him to lurch forward. The soldier's pistol discharged as he fell, the pellet ricocheting harmlessly through the branches overhead.

Dozens of villagers began to plow onto the scene, many of them with bows drawn and muskets ready. They stopped the moment they reached the clearing, however, seeing only a wounded but standing Young John, two wounded and one dead British soldier, a badly beaten Tuck, and Lucy, standing with a smoking musket in her hand.

Young John grabbed Fitzwater by his blonde hair and dragged the screaming and bloody British officer into the center of the clearing, tossing him against a cowering, terrified Wilkes.

As the Mohawk villagers closed in on the men, Kana Kó:re tapped Lucy on the shoulder. *"We must find Kaweh-*

nákens," she said.

Lucy lowered the musket she still held and nodded anxiously at her sister. She then followed Kana Kó:re in the direction of the crevice. After examining the shredded bonds at the base of the large oak tree, Lucy carefully crept to the edge of the crevice and looked down. At the bottom of the rock formation, near the jagged mouth of the valley below, Kawehnákens lay, her arms and legs splayed at unnatural angles. A white man lay next to her.

Lucy let out an earsplitting scream.

Kana Kó:re crawled to the edge next to her sister. "Kawehnákens!" she yelled.

The little girl at the base of the crevice quivered and turned her head slightly. She was alive.

"We have to get down there, Tekawí:iaks," Kana Kó:re said, looking Tekawí:iaks directly in the eyes. *"She's hurt. We must make her well."*

Lucy nodded and turned around, her back now facing the mouth of the crevice. She reached down with her foot and felt for a solid foothold. *"The face is rigid,"* she said. *"We can climb down."*

"No," Kana Kó:re said, pointing to a spot about a hundred meters to the south of the crevice. *"The valley wall bends upward over there. We can walk down."*

Lucy looked up and saw that the spot where Kana Kó:re was pointing looked more like a hill. She was relieved to see it, not just because it would make getting down that much easier, but also because she did not want to think about how they would get an injured Kawehnákens back up the sheer face of a rocky crevice.

The two girls tiptoed around the mouth of the crevice and then sprinted for the hill. As their feet reached the bottom of the valley, Lucy noticed that the grass there was still lush and green and that the soil was quite moist. Her fur-lined moccasins sloshed through the muddy ground, carrying her quickly to Kawehnákens' side.

"*Are you okay, little one?*" Kana Kó:re asked, her voice rife with both concern and anger.

Kawehnákens moaned in pain and clutched at her side.

Lucy could see that the little girl was badly injured. It looked as though every bone in her body had been broken. Nevertheless, she managed to scoop Kawehnákens into her arms and carry her swiftly back to the clearing.

With the help of Kana Kó:re, Lucy carefully placed her little sister on the ground beneath Young John's feet. Until the arrival of his injured daughter, the proud Mohawk had been standing guard over the whimpering whites, deciding the best course of action. Since Young John's daughter was the one who had been taken, tribal custom dictated that he should determine the fate of her kidnappers. However, these men were British and his nation was allied to the men in the red coats. Thus, they should be taken to the British for justice. These men however, were not in uniform and every part of Young John's being called for revenge. The villagers simply awaited Young John's orders.

"*Oh, my beautiful daughter,*" Young John said, kneeling down and placing his lips on Kawehnákens' forehead. Just by the look of her, the Mohawk could tell that she would not survive. Her body was limp and bleeding, and her breathing ragged.

Suddenly, the proud man's face tightened, and he turned his attention to Lucy. "*Tekawí:iaks,*" he said, "*These men must explain. You speak their language. Will you translate?*"

"*I will,*" Lucy said, stifling a sob as she gazed down at her quivering sister.

"*Ask them why they did this,*" Young John said,

standing again and motioning to Wilkes and Hamilton.

"My father would like to know why you have done this," Lucy said to the men. She looked Wilkes in the eyes, and at that moment, almost fell to her knees by the sense that she had seen him before – and that the circumstances had been similarly painful. She may not have been able to recall the specific memory, but she knew in her heart that this man had hurt her before.

Wilkes looked up from his kneeling position. A sick smile crossed his face as the blood dribbling from the top of his head, mixed with his sweat, and streamed down the bridge of his nose. "So, you've gone savage," he said. "You're the reason, young lady."

"*He says...*" Lucy began to say to Young John – but then she stopped quickly, realizing what Wilkes had just related.

"What do you mean, *I'm* the reason?" she asked, again addressing Wilkes.

"You mean to say..." Wilkes said. Then, his smile fell slack and the man looked pensive. "You really don't remember, do you?" he said, practically to himself.

"I don't remember you, if that's what you mean," Lucy said defensively, not really willing to believe her own words.

"*What is he saying, Tekawí:iaks?*" Young John interjected.

"*He says that I am the reason that they have come.*"

"*What does that mean?*"

"*That is what I am trying to find out.*"

Lucy, her brow furrowed, bent down to within inches of the kneeling man's face. "What don't I remember?" she asked.

Wilkes scoffed. One of the men from the village, apparently taking offense to Wilkes' insolence, lightly rapped the white man on the back of the head with his club. Wilkes lurched forward, but then laughed. "I can't believe I've tracked you this far and you don't even remember who I am," he said.

"Who are you?"

Wilkes was practically hysterical at this point. A few of the men reared back with their weapons to beat him again, but Young John signaled for them to stand down.

"My name is Wilkes. Charles Wilkes. Ring any bells?"

Lucy delved deep into her mind, but could not recall the name. *"His name is Charles Wilkes,"* she said absently to Young John.

"Months ago, you were captured by British forces during your attempt to run guns for the American rebels," Wilkes continued.

Lucy translated for her father, who looked both amazed and deeply troubled by the information.

"You were placed in my command and were being led to the nearest British stronghold to be tried for treason." Wilkes then slumped down on his knees. Talking about this topic seemed to enrage him. He spoke with darkening eyes and a hollow tone. "But en route, a violent storm rolled in and several of my prisoners, including you, escaped in the confusion."

"I escaped capture from the British," Lucy said to Young John, not sure whether to be proud or terribly troubled by this revelation. She settled on troubled since, no matter how much Wilkes elaborated, she could not recall a single detail of her apparently daring escape.

"What else do you know?" Lucy pleaded to Wilkes. "Do you know my name?"

Wilkes laughed even harder than before. "You don't even know your name?" he said.

Lucy looked at the ground, trying her best not to cry. "No, Mr. Wilkes. I don't remember *anything.*"

Wilkes straightened up again. He seemed to be doing his best to look certain death proudly in the face. He stared at Young John and said, "Tell these savages to spare my life and I'll tell you your name."

Lucy froze. She did not know what to do. On the one hand, she wanted desperately to learn her name. On the other, she knew that she could never trust this man. Even if he did reveal a name, how could she know if it was the truth?

"What is he saying, Tekawí:iaks?" Kana Kó:re asked, resting her hand on her sister's shoulder.

"Nothing," Lucy said, quivering as she spoke the word. "I don't believe you," she said to Wilkes. "I don't remember much about my past, but I do remember that you have mistreated many people. I will not ask that you be harmed, but I refuse to give you the opportunity to save your life, either."

Wilkes' smile faded. Turning his gaze back to Young John, Wilkes' face seemed to grow slack. The distinct look of shamed agony shined dully from behind his eyes.

"An eye for an eye? Well then, I'm glad the girl was hurt," Wilkes said, glaring blankly at Kawehnákens.

Lucy turned her attention to her younger sister. Kawehnákens was still breathing, if shallowly. Deny it though she might, Lucy had to admit to herself that Wilkes was right. Barring a miracle, the little girl was as good as dead.

"That's all he has for us, Father," Lucy said.

"Why did he hurt Kawehnákens?" Young John asked. *"What reason could he possibly have?"*

Lucy's eyes began to fill with tears. *"To get to me,"* she said. The horror of the realization hit her like a thunderclap. All she could think to do was run out of the clearing

– and she did so quickly, slowing to a trot once she was out of sight of the rest of the villagers. She began sobbing loudly after she had put a little more distance between herself and the scene.

At that moment, she felt more alone than she ever had in her life. The feeling was short-lived, however, as she noticed the soft touch of Kana Kó:re's hand on her shoulder. She turned and looked into the face of her sister, her former rival. Kana Kó:re was crying, too. The two young ladies embraced.

Several of the villagers were championing to dispatch the prisoners.

"They tried to kill your daughter," one of the men said.

"She may not survive," another added.

Young John thought deeply on the matter. As much as he would have liked to allow the others to kill his enemy, he simply felt that he should not. *"These men are British, not Mohawk,"* he said. *"According to our alliance with the white king, they should be brought before their own kind to be tried for this injustice."*

The men closest to the captive soldiers groaned. One of them kicked Fitzwater in the back, causing him to roll forward. A moment of chaos followed. As the private struggled to his knees, Wilkes scrambled forward to grab the musket out of a nearby Mohawk's hands. He managed to wrench the gun free and turned to fire at Young John. Before he could shoot, however, another of the villagers clubbed him from behind. Wilkes fell limply to the ground.

Young John turned to pick up his youngest daughter. He tried to ignore the fact that she was not breathing. Maybe if he pretended that she was still alive, he reasoned, he could hold his tears until he was out of sight of the other men. As he turned, his daughter's limp body lying across his heavy forearms, he nodded to the men who now stood over Wilkes and Fitzwater.

As the proud Mohawk reached the underbrush and slipped out of the clearing, he could see his other two daughters ahead. Still locked in an embrace, both of them seemed to buckle beneath the weight of their pain.

Lucy and Kana Kó:re turned their attention to their approaching father, crying harder as they saw that Kawehnákens was no longer conscious. As Kana Kó:re placed the back of her hand against her younger sister's forehead, the sound of the villagers clubbing Wilkes and his private was dulled by the pounding of their broken hearts.

Kana Kó:re then looked squarely into Lucy's tearful eyes. At that moment, both young women were bonded together forever, each of them realizing that the other was the only sister they had left.

Chapter Sixteen

François

Point Levis, Canada, November 1775

IT WAS WELL KNOWN by the Americans that there was no love lost between the French Canadians and the British. It had been prearranged by General Schuyler that a small group of Canadians, led by a man named François, would recruit a huge number of like-minded men to join up with Arnold's troops and together open a second front, drawing the British from the colonies. Unfortunately a large number of the Canadian population was not willing to assist the American invaders. François' men numbered one hundred and seventy-five and they had been waiting patiently at the head of the Chaudière River for Arnold and his men. The British knew François and placed a large reward for his capture. If he had a ship, then he would have been a most dangerous pirate. As it was, on land, he was a most dangerous highwayman and rebel. François had lost two brothers during the fight for Quebec and his whole family had been uprooted from their homes for their participation in aiding the French army. His motive for joining with the Americans was not so much that he liked them; he just hated the British more. While getting France back into Canada did not seem realistic, he believed his rights would be more secure under the American system.

It was early afternoon when the first of the Americans began to appear -- a rag-tag group of men that had just completed the most arduous journey they could have imagined. They had lost over two hundred of their comrades to hunger and exhaustion. Compounding the effort, over two hundred more had deserted and returned home. As more and more men began to appear, it was clear to François that the line of men still stretched further back.

The Americans approached the Canadians with caution. These were tumultuous times and trust was a scarce commodity. Trust could get you captured or killed.

"Alors," he shouted, "Where is your Colonel Arnold?"

Will Ashley moved up the line with his musket drawn and beaded on the Frenchman. "He'll be here directly," responded Will. "Who are you?"

The man chuckled a little bit at the brashness of this young man. How could this pup realize the effort it took to keep a hundred and seventy five men together for so long? How could he not realize that he was François and that he could cut him down where he stood, should he so desire? Then he thought on their journey and the difficulties that they encountered and gave this young man quarter. "I am François, my friend and I have been waiting for your Arnold for some time now," he responded.

"He's coming up," said Will. "You boys got any food you can spare?"

The Americans looked drawn and emaciated. François turned to his men and said, *"Attend to the Yankees. Get them some food."*

His men responded by bringing over whatever food they could spare. François also sent a few men out to see what game they could hunt down.

Morgan arrived from the rear. "The others are a little ways back and they're in a bad way," he said. Rubbing his hand on his grubby trousers, he extended it to François. "I'm Morgan."

"Un plaisir," the Canadian responded. "We shall send out some men to bring in the others."

"I was told there would be an army waiting for us," Morgan said.

"And I was told there would be an army coming up to meet us," responded François sarcastically.

"We lost a lot of men trying to get here."

"As did we. Perhaps it was not to be, eh? Maybe you should go back."

Before another word could be spoken, Benedict Arnold made his appearance. "We appreciate your efforts, François. It's good to see you."

"And you. You will be pleased to know, Colonel, that your Montgomery will probably take Montreal and now it seems you and I will take Quebec," he said. He looked at the two Americans a little warily. *Was he helping to replace one conqueror for another?*

Arnold did not think he would be smiling again, but

word of Montgomery gave him a reason for doing so. "It certainly seems that way, François. It certainly seems so."

On November 12th, Montgomery captured Montreal and a day later Benedict Arnold crossed the St Lawrence.

Chapter Seventeen

Passage

Mohawk Valley, NY, November 1775

THOUGH IT STILL PAINED her greatly, Lucy was beginning to cope with life without Kawehnákens. The snows had arrived and the land was covered with a pristine, bright-white blanket. Unlike the political climate of the Canadian territory, the land seemed at peace, but only on the surface. She had heard from the trappers and traders passing through earlier that month that the revolution was still in full vigor, and that the Americans were close to walking into Montreal, but at least for now the Mohawks could take the time to enjoy their families and tend to their many village matters.

Lucy sat on an old log by the riverbank, studying a thin stream of water. The river was icing over and only a narrow opening remained. The flowing water, having been channeled through an open crevice, caused the flow to move very swiftly.

Soon, Lucy thought, *this too will freeze over and blend with the rest of the icy countryside.*

As she looked down at the unrelenting stream she saw an ice covered blue green stone. It shimmered in the sunlight, and suddenly the sounds of footsteps echoed in her memory. Before she could realize that she had slipped into another one of her visions, the running water began taking on shapes that she could not define. Lucy wept as she battled to understand another of her detachments from reality.

Despite her overwhelming desire to believe otherwise, she knew that she was not really the person she had come to be. She was not Tekawí:iaks. She was not Marie. Painfully, she realized that, without even knowing her true name, she was essentially looking at her life from the outside, like a spectator in a game she had long wanted to quit.

Despite the fact that her feet remained firmly planted on the ground, Lucy could sense that she was running.

In her dreamlike state, she was running faster now, feeling her feet hitting the ground with each step. The trees moved away from her as she sprinted between them, darting around the low-lying branches. She could smell the fresh, damp leaves and feel the sting of the pine needles as she brushed by. The thunder behind her echoed in her ears over and over again.

Desperately trying to fend off the branches with her flailing arms, she turned and looked behind her, and saw the distorted shapes of a red line. Billows of white smoke mushrooming in her direction chased her further into the forest. Through the haze lunged the image of a man barking muffled commands as he swung a sword in front of him, hacking at the branches impeding his progress.

Lucy could see the man more clearly now. He had the same sense of imposing evil that the man from her previous dreams had carried, but this time, he was different. He eyes drifted from the glinting blade of the man's sword to his face. She gasped as, for the first time, there was a real face applied to the man. It was Wilkes. All along, it had been Wilkes, she realized – though she was not sure if she believed the notion entirely.

As she turned to run away, part of her wanted to return and ask why.

Why are you trying to kill me?

Who am I?

Dozens of questions came springing to mind, and she wished that she had asked them when she had had the chance. But Lucy had been trained to survive and she knew that she could not go back.

After a few long minutes of struggling through the trees, she flung another glance over her shoulder at her attacker. To her amazement, the face that scowled back at her was no longer that of Wilkes. This man was gaunt and pale, his eyes black and sunken. A fresh wave of terror swept over her, and Lucy knew she would never want to be caught by this man. Even though she did not recognize the features, she knew that she shared an ugly history with him.

Frightened, Lucy faced forward again and, at that moment, plowed headlong into a darkened tunnel. Inside was utter silence and darkness. All Lucy could hear was her heart beating; all she could see was the black pall all around her. Her mind screamed for her to stop before she ran into something or fell into a hole, but instinct propelled her forward, fearing her attacker far more than the uncertainty of what lay ahead.

And so she charged forward into the dark, further and further into the depths of her forgotten memory. The further she ran, the colder the cave became. Vapor from her hot breath met the cold air and rose up before her eyes like white smoke against the backdrop of sheer black. As she advanced further, the rising white vapor began to crystallize in the now-crippling cold.

Tiny shards of the ice froze the air in front of her face. After a few moments of studying the shards, Lucy realized two things. First, these shards were not ice at all. They were glass. And second, although she was out of breath and her heart pounded madly, she was no longer running. In fact, her feet seemed anchored to the ground.

Looking down, she saw a wooden window-frame floating into view as though carried by an unseen hand. The shards of crystalline glass became larger as the windowpane drew near. When the window paused in front of her, Lucy could see the image of a person on the other side -- a young girl holding a musket.

Lucy gasped as she realized that the face in the window was her own.

Not wanting to face the harsh revelation any longer, Lucy turned to look back in the direction from which she had come. She saw nothing. When she looked forward again, the girl was gone. Except for a dim, yellow glow in the distance, there was only darkness once again.

Suddenly, her feet kicked up again. She was free from the ground and able to move forward. Just as before, she ran, only this time in the direction of the yellowish glow.

After what felt like miles, she drew up next to the source of the glow, a small fire crackling in a makeshift rock pit.

The young lady involuntarily sat down on a nearby log and warmed herself. The warmth was wonderful and soothing. She closed her eyes for a few seconds.

She was startled out of her brief reverie by the sound of a burning piece of wood snapping. She opened her eyes.

As she looked into the fire, Lucy could sense someone sitting beside her. She turned and could see the clear image of a boy she once knew. *Will Ashley.* Both the name and the vision of the boy were fleeting, however. She blinked and both were gone.

Suddenly, the fire dimmed and the cold returned.

Lucy felt herself rising to her feet once more. The space that now surrounded her was dark and confined. Her arms were heavy.

Looking down, she could see that she was carrying several muskets under her arms. She moved forward, placing them down in a corner against a cold, clay-like wall. Lucy turned to the light emanating from what she perceived to be the entrance to this cave – and, she hoped, the exit to this nightmare. She bolted in the direction of the light, almost falling as she stumbled over a pile of muskets.

As she got closer to the light, she could hear the rushing water. Sunlight flashed all around her as she exited onto the cold, snow-covered ground and sat down on a log near the running water.

In a blink, she realized that she was back at the river-bank. Moments later, she understood that the nightmare had ended – only it seemed as though she had not actually slept. More than anything, Lucy wanted to understand what was happening to her, but knew with a heavy heart that this knowledge was not yet hers to gain…yet. Frustrated and confused, Lucy wept.

Young John crept silently up behind his daughter as he listened to the sound of her crying.

"*What is it you see, my daughter?*" he asked as he gently put his hands on Lucy's shoulders and stared at the river with her.

"*Am I?*" Lucy replied, lifting her arm up and touching Young John's hand.

"*Are you what?*"

"*Am I your daughter?*" Lucy cried harder as she spoke the words. One side of her longed to give up her past and pretend that Young John was actually all that she had ever known of a father. The other wanted to run away from this kindly Mohawk – into the woods and in search of her true identity.

Young John shrugged knowingly. He had long sensed his daughter's struggle. "*I call you Tekawí:iaks,*" he said. "*Les Français call you Marie. Whatever you are called, you are his child.*" Young John pointed to the sky as he spoke these last words. "*The Great One has brought you to us. You have survived where many others have fallen.*"

Lucy cried silently, wondering if she deserved such a fate.

"*Life is a passage,*" Young John continued. "*A portage that takes you to the end by means of many different paths. In time, you will come to accept yourself as you are now and what you will become later. Whoever you are, for now, you are with us. And as long as you are with us, you are my daughter.*"

"*But I am not like you,*" Lucy responded.

Young John smiled and placed his hand on Lucy's head. "*Young one, you are more like us than you know. We care for you. You are family.*"

Lucy chuckled as she wiped away her tears. "*Tell that to Kana Kó:re,*" she said with a smile.

Young John smiled back. *"Oh, come now,"* he said. *"I saw the two of you in the forest. You were embracing."*

Lucy shook her head. *"It's so hard."*

"I know my daughter. She respects you. You are both growing women. As such, it is in Kana Kó:re's nature as a growing woman to be a little jealous...and yours," he added. *"Especially around Ahentáken."* Young John smiled as he touched Lucy's slender nose.

"I know it's been decided that he and Kana Kó:re will be together one day," Lucy said. *"But I can't change the fact that he finds me interesting."*

"Kana Kó:re knows that also. That is why, in time, you will become as close as you are..." Young John shook his head, correcting himself. *"As you* were *with Kawehnákens."*

The proud Mohawk then got up and walked back toward the village. Looking back over his shoulder, he added, *"Time changes everything. In time, you will know who you are...even if it takes the rest of your lifetime to find the answers."*

Chapter Eighteen

Québec

Quebec City, Canada, November 1775

SAVE FOR ITS SOUTHERNMOST flank, Quebec was a city surrounded completely by fortified walls. The entrance gate stood on a higher elevation than the rest of the city, overlooking Lower Town, a district of houses and government blockhouses, shops, and other commerce. To the southeast of the city was the St. Lawrence River. To the north was the St. Charles. Directly to the east were the St. Johns and the Plains of Abraham. This walled city was simple compared to most European structures, but was nonetheless a battle-tested fortress.

By this point, it was already common knowledge in the city that Fort Montreal had surrendered to Montgomery and the small band of Canadians serving with him. The defeat was certainly a painful blow to the British forces – and came as particularly bad news to those manning this stronghold of Quebec. But the victory had certainly weakened Montgomery's forces, so much so that a continued independent advance almost seemed beyond the realm of possibility.

Shortly after news of this landmark loss reached the town walls, another bit of helpful reconnaissance was brought to light.

Guy Carleton, the Governor of Quebec, after relinquishing Montreal and receiving news of Arnold's invasion route, hurried to Quebec disguised as a farmer to inform the military men within his borders of the impending siege. Upon his arrival, he ordered the crews aboard the H.M.S. Lizard and H.M.S. Hunter – who were docked in the St. Lawrence, preparing the ships for the harsh Canadian winter – to remove many of the cannons and bring them to the city. Also, every able-bodied man was to make himself available for service within the city walls.

Later, a general named MacLean visited the office of Governor Carleton, bringing his superior officer up to speed on his preparations for the defense of the city. The office was painted from top to bottom in a painfully stark white. It was a high-ceiling affair with wooden accoutrements and wide tables on which to lay and examine maps. The amenities were perfect for this particular occasion, as Carleton squeezed his generous girth around the corner of the central table and gazed down upon a map of the region surrounding the city in which he made quarter.

"Awful news about Montreal, sir. It seems the rebels will most likely want repeat their strategy by laying siege to this city…" MacLean said, pointing to the area south of Quebec. "That is until Montgomery gets here from Montreal, sir."

MacLean was a proud man with wide, English jowls and a rather flat face. Behind this rather unflattering countenance was a simple but effective military mind.

"Tut, MacLean," Carleton replied dismissively. "What would possess their commander to be so bold?" He gestured to the lines on the map marking the city's walls and other strongholds. "We have fortifications, the cannons, and now with the seamen and marines supplementing some of our less experienced soldiers, we have men enough to repel twice the force that he can muster."

MacLean sighed deeply, running his hands down his bright red jacket to his tight, starched, obscenely white pants.

"Arnold wants to draw us out, I imagine," he said.

"But why on earth would we let him do that?"

"See, that's just it. Basically, I agree, Governor. Remaining in the city is our best option. We can wait it out. We're in a war of attrition. The weather will be against them. They won't be able to hold siege for long."

Carleton furrowed his brow. Though the plan was simple, something did not quite seem to be clicking for him yet.

"They'll have to attack then. What about Montgomery?" he finally said. "When is he expected?"

"He's not too far behind. He should be here within a fortnight."

Carleton paced to the corner of the room and pensively examined a completely irrelevant map of the Virginia. He ran his stubby fingers across his flabby chin and sighed deeply once again. "And his troops won't be many?"

"No, sir. Why?"

"Well, I mean...he won't provide Arnold with the boost his men will need?"

"No, sir. We expect Montgomery's forces to be less

than five hundred strong."

"Good God, man." Carleton looked incredulous, a devilish smile revealing a set of yellowed, crooked teeth. "If they attack, it will be their ruin."

Within the week, Benedict Arnold and his men had arrived upon Quebec. Of his original force of over 1,200 men, less than 700 remained. The combination of cold weather, starvation, fever, and desertion had depleted the ranks into a grossly inadequate force.

Despite the odds being stacked against him, Arnold proudly sent his messengers to the gates of Quebec City with a direct ultimatum: surrender or fight.

What Arnold had not counted on was the fact that the British had heard word of his immanent arrival several days earlier. As was the case, they were already fully prepared for such a measure – and were quite secure in their positions. As Carleton had ordered, despite the challenge from Arnold, they would hold back and wait, studying this bold but outnumbered enemy.

Ben White and Will Ashley sat in the snow on an embankment near the St. Charles River, where the rebel forces had come to set up camp. Both were shivering uncontrollably – a feeling that Will had grown quite used to. In fact, the act of shivering had become so commonplace that he had ceased to notice that it was even happening. The only real indication that he was doing it was the fact that Ben was shaking right before his eyes.

"Cold, Ben?" Will asked, a chapped smile forming over his chattering teeth.

"Nah, I seen worse," Ben said, blowing air into his folded hands.

"Oh yeah? When was that?"

"Back in '60, I think it was. '61, maybe."

Will laughed and slapped his knee, which had been numb due to the cold for as long as he could remember. "You were two years old in '60."

"Well, then, maybe it was '62...I don't know."

Will smiled and lay back in the snow. Despite the unbearable cold, it felt good to lay on something soft for a change. He could hear the familiar sound of Ben rubbing his hands together, trying to warm them up.

"When you think we'll get our orders?" Ben asked dreamily.

"Soon," Will said without hesitation.

"What makes you say that?"

Will sat back up, looking out into the distance. The walls of Quebec seemed to loom above the horizon. They were the largest things he had ever seen. It was an ominous sight – a fortified and heavily manned city that seemed to be suspended in water – but Will knew in his heart that he would find glory in that place. "Well, my friend," Will said, "In case you hadn't noticed, it's mighty cold outside."

"You're right," Ben said, laughing. "I hadn't noticed."

Will smiled.

"So you figure that means we'll get the orders soon?"

"I don't now how it could be any other way. Look around you, Ben. More men are dying every day. Those that don't die from the cold are walking off in search of warmth. Our only chance to survive is to get into that city. So our only chance of making it out alive is to attack and to attack soon."

Ben attempted to whistle, but his lips were so chapped and frozen that he could not make the noise.

As frustration set in, Arnold made good on Will's

prediction. With confidence in his men, he ordered a night attack in the hopes of testing the British strength and will to fight.

The skirmish would last for little more than a few hours, with the fortified British essentially lobbing all the cannon-fire they had at the approaching rabble. Casualties were few, but the onslaught left Arnold with few choices.

Beaten back, the colonel would withdraw his troops to Point-Aux-Trembles and wait for Montgomery and his men to arrive.

In his now-tattered officer's tent, a small fire crackling in the corner, Arnold stood with Morgan, studying the vulnerable points of the city. Arnold's finger traced over the north flank and then settled upon the south, the only portion of the city that did not feature a wall.

Morgan watched his commander and could imagine what was going through his mind.

"Damn, Morgan," Arnold said. "I so want this place."

"I know you do, sir," Morgan replied. "Montgomery will be here soon and we can move then."

Arnold seemed distant as he crossed to the flickering fire and warmed his hands over the flames. Suddenly he pulled his cap off his head and examined the lining, realizing that it was falling apart at the seams. "I fear that Montgomery's forces won't be enough, Morgan," he said at last.

Morgan did not reply. He, too, had the suspicion that the operation was doomed – but pride and honor propelled him forward.

After a long and uncomfortable silence Arnold wheeled around to face his counterpart, a solemn look in his eye. He replaced the cap onto his head and then grasped Morgan's shoulder with his right hand. "We must keep the men together, Morgan," he said.

The captain nodded and turned sharply to leave. On his way out, he thought about how headstrong and impudent his commanding officer tended to be -- but in this case, he could not help but agree. The only real opportunity to take the city would require waiting for Montgomery. The only trouble was that waiting was the one thing this withering army could not afford to do.

Carleton and MacLean spent the next few days planning for the protection of Quebec. Due to the ever-deteriorating elements, both suspected that the big attack would come soon.

They stood once again in Carleton's opulent office, looking over the same map of the city that they had examined before.

"We have hoisted cannons onto rooftops here and here," MacLean said, pointing out spots on the map. "And onto the top floor of the houses here, here, and here, we also have cannons in place." He then swung his finger down and pointed in the opposite direction. "They can be turned to cover this area, if need be."

"Who've we got on the guns?" Carleton asked. "Canadians?"

MacLean chuckled. "No, sir, the Canadians are barricaded on these streets. They'll serve as the front lines. And reserves are standing by."

Carleton smiled and turned away from the military man. He hooked his left thumb proudly in the pocket of his blue vest. "Well, that's it then," he said.

"That's it, sir."

Chapter Nineteen

Sault au Matelot

Quebec City, Canada, December 1775

MONTGOMERY'S MARCH WAS LONG and slow. A week prior, General Schuyler had been killed. Between the weather and his death, keeping up the morale of the men was a real struggle.

In addition to this serious problem, Montgomery had managed to bring along far fewer soldiers than he had hoped to bring. With the capture of Montreal came the responsibility to hold Montreal – and the general was forced to leave behind enough good men to defend the city.

By the time Montgomery met up with Benedict Arnold on December 3rd, only 350 of his soldiers remained. At that point, none of the frozen, exhausted soldiers realized that their two commanding officers would waste no time in sending them into the fray.

On December 5th the combined forces would lay siege to the city.

—⸙—

Arnold looked over his plans and reviewed his strategy with General Montgomery. It was a strategy he had been building up since long before the general had arrived. "Well, Richard," he said, "they can't move in or out. Essentially, we have them held down."

"Trapped like rats," Montgomery said. "My men have experience with this sort of thing. They fought valiantly at Montreal and they'll do it again."

"Glad to hear it, my good man."

Arnold strolled away from Montgomery, an expression of painful obligation lighting in his eyes. After he'd gone about five paces, he turned back around to face his new brother in arms. "We've been here for weeks now, Richard, but we can't stay forever."

"I know, Benedict," Montgomery said. "My men feel the pain of the cold as well. We need to get inside those walls. We'll have to take the city."

"And we *need* to take it soon. That's a critical stronghold. Overtaking it could well turn the tide in our favor in this little war."

Montgomery remained silent. The shivering lieutenant in the corner of the tent, attempting to inch closer to the fire, diverted his attention.

Arnold followed Montgomery's gaze.

"Oh, Squires," he said. "I'm glad you're here." He then turned to Montgomery. "Tea, Richard?" he asked.

Montgomery shook his head.

"Well, never mind then, Lieutenant," Arnold said.

"Anyway, warm yourself by the fire, my boy."

The lieutenant wasted no time in doing as he was told. He rushed over to the fire and began warming his hands.

Arnold turned his attention back to Montgomery. "Of course, it would be easier on us if they came out to fight, but MacLean's a smart commander. I imagine that the old devil will wait us out, study us, and then decide on the best course of action for his men to take. If not, an attack on our part is inevitable. We either succeed or fail come the end of December."

Montgomery was not sure, but he could have sworn that he saw the lieutenant perk up at the mention of a timeframe. He pondered the idea of the end of December for a moment, then his face brightened a little. "Enlistments," he said.

"Enlistments," Arnold agreed. "As you obviously know, on January 1st, the enlistment for many of our men comes to an end. If we hope to maintain the forces we have left, we must strike before that comes to pass."

Montgomery let out an odd little groan.

"So, my friend," Arnold continued, "let us plan the attack and hope that the Brits break down before we do."

"Agreed. Let's hope they come out to fight us head on."

"All right, then, Richard. I've been having a look at this map for quite some time – since we took up our post here in Quebec, in fact. Now, François and his men will make a diversionary attack at the north wall, which hopefully will draw their fire. While he does that, I propose that we move your three hundred men to attack the southern part of the city. It is the weakest point and should be the most logical place to send the smaller arm of our forces. I shall lead my men from the north, where you and I will meet here and move into the city."

Have I faced starvation and disease only to get to die in this strange place?

Will I ever see my family again?

These thoughts and others had haunted John Squires for some time now. Winter and time had changed him -- made him a different man. As he skulked to the gate of the city under cover of night, he convinced himself that Arnold would get him and the rest the Americans killed if he was allowed to proceed unimpeded with his hopeless plan.

As far as Squires was concerned, he was not about to be included in the casualties of this ridiculous siege. Still, up until that very moment that he walked through the door to Governor Carleton's office, doubts plagued him.

Don't do this, Johnny. Give up, sure, but don't do this, he told himself over and over again.

The American deserter stood in front of Guy Carleton's desk under heavy guard. General MacLean was among them.

Carleton smiled. "I hear you have something to tell us, Lieutenant Squires," he said.

Think of all the lives you'll save, Squires told himself for the hundredth time, hoping to work up as much courage as possible before making either the best or worst decision of his entire life. Little did he know that the outcome of an entire war could ride on the back of a few simple words.

Overcoming the reservations that remained in his heart, Squires informed Carleton of Arnold's intention to attack.

Without saying another word to the deserter – not even a thank you for his contribution – Carleton threw everything aside and ordered that the commanders of his forces be informed.

Ben and Will received the bad news the following morning. Though they had marched many miles together and survived what seemed like an insurmountable journey alongside one another, they would now be split up. For the first time, their orders would take them in opposite directions.

Ben and a few others would be attached to Montgomery's group, rounding off his company to three hundred men.

"Tough luck, Benny," Will said, slapping his friend on the shoulder. "But you and I will have a drink together in the town square once we take the city."

Will looked sadly at his friend, who remained silent and pensive. He seemed to want to speak, though he obviously could not find the words.

"Over a roaring fire," Will added jovially.

Ben chuckled politely, but still did not speak.

After another awkward minute of waiting, Will had to ask. "Something wrong, Ben?"

"Will," Ben said, as if snapped out of a dream, "you remember how once I told you about my uncle Ethan? How he got himself killed when he chopped down that big old pine tree?"

"Yeah," Will replied. "That tree just fell on top of him."

"Well, we all thought it was strange that a man could get killed that way. I mean, he could have run away in the other direction, but he just stood there, still and not knowin' what to do."

"What're you sayin' this for, Ben?"

"Will, I was with him when he chopped the tree. I didn't move either; I just stood there too. That's how I come to lose parta my ear. It was a tree branch from that tree, not a British musket ball. I'm kinda feelin' the same way right now, too. I know somethin's gonna happen and I feel like I'm standin' here with no choice. Feel like I'm just waitin' to die."

"Aw, Ben, you'll be all right. Montgomery is one of the best we got, I hear. You just follow him and keep your head down, and you'll come out all right."

"I wish I believed you, Will. I surely do."

Quebec City, December 28, 1775

It was approximately one o'clock in the morning and final preparations were being discussed for the imminent attack on the last British bastion in Canada. The Americans controlled all the country except for Quebec. With Carleton were British Colonel Henry Caldwell and Canadian Militia Colonel Noel Voyer.

"Gentlemen," Carleton said, "we have information that, if correct, will virtually assure us the attack will occur within the next day or two. It seems that many of the rebel troops' enlistments will be up come the first of the year. Montgomery and Arnold will need to strike by then if they are to have any sort of hope of breaching the walls. What do you think Voyer?"

"With the ships' cannon here and on the rooftops here and here, we have created a devastating field of fire, sir."

"Then so be it," Carleton said. "Make them run Voyer. Make them run!"

The stage was set for the attack and defense of the city. Inside the city, 357 regulars, 450 seamen, 543 Canadians, and 300 militiamen stood ready to face Arnold's force of 900 cold and hungry troops.

Pres de Ville, Canada, December 31, 1775

An omen, thought Montgomery as he and his men

were pummeled by a surprise snowstorm as they prepared to assault Fort Quebec. As cold as they were, his 300 men were in high spirits, hoping the battle would end quickly, thus ending the hardships they had suffered since September.

Make the best from the worst, Montgomery thought. *Maybe the surprise is ours...hidden by the weather.*

As planned, the troops moved out along the coastline at 4 A.M. Their objective was to overtake a blockhouse at Pres de Ville. Inside the blockhouse, Captain Chabot and Lieutenant Picard, along with sailors from the Lizard and thirty Canadian militiamen, were ready and waiting.

In the distance, barely audible because of the howling wind, were the raps of sporadic musket fire. *François was right on schedule,* thought Montgomery.

Montgomery led his men, pressing forward in the driving blizzard, advancing along the coastline past Cape Diamond Bastion and eventually arriving at the blockhouse. To slow the attack, the protectors had hastily built a barricade.

Inside, the command was given and seamen gunners fired the first salvo of grapeshot. Militia fired their muskets in unison, clearing a swath of Americans and killing Montgomery instantly. Ben Weaver, along with a dozen others, was also killed. The remaining Americans locked their sights on the blockhouse, but most were unable to fire. With their barrels clogged with ice and snow, their muskets were rendered useless. They had no choice but to turn back in haste. The southern attack on the city was over almost as quickly as it had begun.

Sault au Matelot, Quebec City, December 31, 1775
Advancing off the northern wall of the city, Arnold could hear the explosions of the musket-fire coming from

the direction of Pres de Ville.

Sounds like Montgomery is giving them hell, he thought.

"Let's keep it going!" Arnold yelled.

Will was moving close by Benedict Arnold, cupping his hand over the hammer and flint of his musket. The cold cut right through him, but he kept moving in the direction of a street barricade just ahead.

Will noticed the street sign "Sault au Matelot" on the side of the corner building. He saw nothing moving from the barricade and thought it to be a roadblock. He kept thinking of Ben's Uncle Ethan.

I know now what old Ben was trying to tell me, he thought.

The thought vanished, however, the moment the Canadian militia, who had waited patiently for the invaders, opened fire. Will and the others advanced under fire until they came to the side of the barricade.

A musket ball hit Arnold in his foot, reducing his walk to a hobble. Arnold grabbed hold of Morgan as he advanced behind him. "Keep it going, Morgan," was his last command to his most trusted officer.

Will and another soldier carried Arnold to the rear as Daniel Morgan prepared to move forward. Will moved Arnold swiftly, as he wanted to rejoin the men in the glory they all thought would be theirs.

Morgan managed to capture the barricade, meeting the first objective of the mission. Another group of Americans carried ladders and gained entry into a second floor house. From there, they provided covering fire to Morgan holding at the barricade.

Unsure of what to do next, Morgan delayed the attack. Grabbing hold of another man, he ordered him back to inform Arnold of their success and to get further orders.

The words had no sooner left his mouth when men of the Royal Highland Emigrants, Highlanders, and Canadians, retook the second floor and began firing at the rebels below. They were pinned down.

Morgan ordered a retreat, but in the blinding storm, a number of the men lost their way. All the men could hear was the thumping of boots on the snow-covered street as the Canadian militia rushed forward, routing the Americans and pursuing them out of the city.

A British counterattack led by Colonel Allen McLean then recaptured the barricade, leaving the Americans in the middle of the Canadians and the British.

Arnold instinctively knew the inevitable outcome as he watched some of his panicked troops returning and gathering around his makeshift headquarters.

The battle ended at 10 A.M. with Daniel Morgan surrendering alongside his men.

To: George Washington

Sir,

It is with regret that I am to inform you that our assault on Quebec was repelled.

Our forces suffered the loss of Major General Richard Montgomery, 65 men also killed and 430 taken as prisoners.

I have not surrendered my position and it is my intention to hold and lay siege as long as possible or until relieved.

Col. Arnold

Chapter Twenty

Daniel

Mohawk Valley, N.Y. February 1776

THE FULL MOON SHONE brightly in the clear, cloudless sky. The gray-black stones of the houses stood in cold, dark contrast to the pure, white snow that covered the ground. A light wind lifted the white powder off the ground, carrying the snow in every direction.

The light of the moon and the snow-dust hitting the window near where she slept awakened Lucy. It was around three in the morning when she opened her eyes.

"Emy?" she asked, speaking a name that just seemed to leave her mouth on its own.

Getting to her feet, she walked past her sister and made her way to the door. The static sound of the snow hitting the windows and door seemed to carry words that she could just make out.

"Lucy," she heard, "all is well."

She cracked the door open and gazed upon the moonlit ground. The snow billowed and swirled in a dance of confusion, moving away from her. The cold air bit into her body, but she remained focused on the movement outside. The snow began to take the shape of a man and a woman walking away arm in arm. The shapes looked familiar, but she could not place them.

The shapes stopped, turned to face her. She could see the faces a little clearer now, which made them seem more familiar still. The speed at which the snow swirled about increased, and the snow dust began to sparkle brightly. The hissing wind moved all around them and whispered, "Be well, daughter." The shapes disappeared instantly, leaving only the sound of the wind.

Lucy returned to her bed, feeling somewhat contented and comforted by the words she had just heard. She also remembered Young John telling her about her passage and that she would be who she is and that, in time, her answers would come.

Later that same morning, a bit east of the Bigelow farm, the red morning sun was just cresting the wooded hills. The air was crisp and pure as the blue hues of the starlit sky indicated that a new day was beginning. The full moon held on in clear view for all to observe its magnificence. Surrounding the farmhouse, new fallen snow stretched for as far as the eye could see, giving evidence of the visitors who had arrived a few hours ago. Wagon tracks and hoof-prints detailed the chosen path of the riders.

The horses were tied as close to the house as possible in

order to protect the animals from the cold, prevailing wind. Aside from the slight whistle of the fast-moving air past some of the timbers, the silence was deafening.

Inside, the fire sparked and snapped wildly in the large kitchen hearth. Seated at the table were Jenny Bigelow, Dr. William Bainbridge, and the good Reverend Moore. Nancy Killgrew had given birth the night before, but things had not gone according to plan.

Jenny sat in silence, her hands wrapped around a hot cup of tea. The baby was resting well, and according to the doctor, he was healthy and would survive. Her thoughts turned to the baby's mother in the next room. The events of the early morning hours tore through her heart as well as her mind.

After the baby's birth the boy was taken away. Jenny noticed Nancy's face and how it seemed transformed by the light of the full moon shinning through the frost-encrusted window. At that moment, Jenny thought back through all of their years of friendship that she and Nancy held so dear. It was all she could do to hold back the tears welling up in her eyes.

"Jenny," Nancy said looking up at her. "How did we come to this? Dear Jenny, I miss my life so."

"What are you saying, dear Nancy?" she asked sitting down at the side of the bed.

"I miss my Tom and Lucy and how things used to be. I can see their faces as clearly as I do yours. The happiness we shared those evenings in my home, their faces basking in the warm glow of the fire."

"I know, my dear. I miss my boy and my man every single day. Each day they are beside me as I do my chores and each evening they kneel with me in prayer."

"Jenny, was it worth it? How will they be remembered?"

"Don't you worry about that now," she said in a scolding tone. "They are patriots and heroes and..." She stopped just in time to choke back her tears. "Well anyway, don't you worry about that now."

Jenny and Nancy looked deep into each other's eyes; their gaze seemed to pierce through their souls. At that moment, they both realized that death would be calling soon.

"Jenny, I want you to promise ..."

"Nancy, you don't have to do this."

"Jenny, I do. Promise me it will be you looking after my son. I entrust him to you and only you. His name shall be Daniel. It was the name my Tom had chosen."

"Now, you'll be lookin' after the wee one yourself. Aye, anyone can see Tom's fierce eyes in the boy," Jenny said forcing a lilt into her voice. "But you know that, don't you."

Tears filled Nancy's eyes. "Yes, I do Jenny, but just in case ... just in case ..."

"You know I will dear friend. You rest now, Nancy. We'll bring the wee one to you in the morning."

Jenny rose from the bedside and walked quietly to the door. Closing it behind her, she raised her apron to her face and wept silently into it. The doctor and the reverend immediately got up to comfort Jenny, offering her a seat at the table.

"Does she need me?" inquired the doctor.

"No, let her rest awhile," Jenny replied, wiping away her tears.

Nancy opened her eyes as the bright moonlight pierced the darkness of her room and fell upon her face. *Emy Moon,* she thought. She looked up to see the beautiful full moon alone in the sky. *Is my Lucy all right?*

Then, as if by some miracle, her face was bathed in a wonderful light. She smiled. "Hello, Tom," she whispered as her husband took shape in the light.

"Oh, Nancy, my beloved wife … how I've missed you," Tom's apparition said.

"And I have missed you, Tom. What of Lucy?"

"Fear not, dear Nancy. Lucy will survive beyond all this, and we will watch over her and our son."

"Why does she not come home, Tom?"

"She cannot, for to come back would surely put her in danger. It is for the best. So fear not. She is in good hands."

"I'm ready, dearest," she said.

"Then take hold of my hand, and we'll away."

Jenny had heard Nancy's voice and opened the door to return to her friend. When she opened the door, Nancy had lifted her hand toward the window as if reaching for something. She looked at Jenny and smiled. Her hand came down to her side and all was still.

"She's gone," Jenny said turning to the men at the table. "Our Nancy has gone."

After Doctor Bainbridge took care of Nancy medically and the good Reverend Moore saw to her spiritually, Jenny saw the two men to their horses. Something had been bothering her, and she wanted to get it off her mind.

"It's strange," she said.

"What's strange, Jenny?" the doctor asked.

"When I walked into Nancy's room that last time, she was smiling." She hesitated for a moment. "Then, when she was gone, it was as if the moonlight shining inside had dimmed and a shadow had moved through what little light there was."

She looked at the doctor. "Someone was there with her," she said, wrapping her shawl close to her. She smiled, "And it gave me hope. Nancy is at peace and with those she loves."

Chapter Twenty-One

An End and Beginning

Mohawk Valley, NY, May, 1776

AS THE SNOW RUNOFF continued its charge down the continent, the Mohawk village was alive with activity. In addition to the spring planting, there was also a good deal of hunting to be done. To Young John, the return of activity was healing; it gave him less time to think.

And then the scout came. A young Mohawk boy who had been trapping and searching near Quebec had galloped in with grave news only three days prior. He held an affinity with Young John; so naturally, he went to him first – even though it was generally the job of the Chief to receive such messages and then the tribal leaders.

"*Troops,*" the boy had said.

"*Yes, there are always troops trekking across our land,*" Young John had offered with a smile. He raised his hand gently in an attempt to calm the boy, who was panting so hard that he seemed ready to pass out at any moment. He had obviously ridden hard for days in his frantic journey.

"*Many troops,*" the boy breathed.

Young John straightened up a bit. Many troops could only mean bad news for a village the size of his – particularly for the Mohawks, whose true role in the wars was often misinterpreted by every side in the conflict. The French and the Americans thought the Mohawks were fully allied with the British, but the British doubted the strength of that alliance.

"*How many troops?*" Young John said, a little more urgently now.

"*Thousands,*" the boy said forcefully.

"*From where do they come?*"

"*A battle. The battle at Quebec fort is over. They are Americans, retreating from the city walls.*"

Young John brought his hand to his chin and thought deeply. He knew very well that his village stood little chance against a hostile army of thousands and he liked almost as little the simple prospect of many foreign forces marching through his land. The natural instinct would be to sound the alarm for a recall of all his fellow tribesmen to gather in preparation for impending attack. The trouble with that particular instinct is that an attack was not necessarily a given. For that reason, thought had to rule the day – and, as such, Young John would need to inform the Chief and tribal leaders and assemble a council to determine the best course of action.

Around a roaring fire they had gathered, the Chief, the four elders including Young John. Several others had come to voice their opinions, as well, but Young John knew that their voices would be barely perceptible above the deep thinking that would take place within this circle.

"Two thousand," Young John said. *"We mark them at a three-day ride from here."*

There was much grumbling among the spectators. Many had come to understand that the whites were never to be trusted – particularly when they assembled in such large groups.

"We send out a recall, then," the youngest of the leaders said. He was a gray-haired man with dark eyes and a droopy mouth. His face was weathered and wrinkled, but still carried an oddly youthful kind of glow. When he spoke, his head often twitched quickly back and forth, as if he were having trouble with invisible flies darting around in front of his face.

Young John hummed his approval. In his heart, though, he felt like calling an army together would be folly. He believed that after such a long siege, the Americans would want to go home to regroup. Still, he could not help but be compelled to protect his family by whatever means necessary. And he knew full well that the Colonials would attack his women, if provoked. Tekawí:iaks, too, did not stand a chance. If she were not killed in the skirmish, the fact that she was white would surely get her taken away with the men to a fate he could not know.

As if he had read Young John's mind, the eldest of the leaders piped softly in. *"That would only provoke them,"* he said. *"If they see our forces gathered, they might attack, regardless of our intentions."*

"So you're saying we are to do nothing?" a young man

yelled from the back of the crowd.

"*I'm saying,*" the elder continued without even looking at the source of the voice, "*that we would do well to appear peaceful. We have not been asked by the Redcoats to intercede. We will be in this war soon enough, and so for the time being, we should do all that we can to stay out of it.*" The old man nodded solemnly as though he were approving his own statements. The feathers in his hair danced beside his elongated, leathery cheeks as he did so.

Young John knew that time would tell if the matter had been settled. The decision may have not reflected the desire of the populace, but he knew there to be a great deal of wisdom in this latest decree. The only way to keep the Colonials out would be to ignore them.

The following day, the nervous village was paid a timely visit by a few old friends. Emile and Simon DuFore had left Montreal a week earlier to begin their trapping season. They, too, brought word, if not a warning, that over eight thousand British and Hessian troops had come to rescue the residents of the fortress city from what was now over two thousand Americans laying siege to its walls. The Americans, they knew, would soon be retreating southward, back to the colonies.

Young John thanked them for their help and their candor and informed them that the tribe had already decided not to take action on the matter.

"I hope you're not making a mistake," Emile said to his old friend.

"That makes two of us, Emile," Young John said seriously.

Simon had grown taller in the year that he had been away from the village. He still looked nothing like his father, but he had managed to grow into an exceptionally handsome young man. He looked far more like a man than a boy this year, as well. His shoulders had broadened and his jaw had descended, growing strong and much more prominent.

Around his waist, just below his rough, pulled-cotton shirt, he wore a belt of dark leather, which he used more as a tie to keep the sheath to his knife at his side than a means to keep his pants from falling off. Unfortunately for Simon, the belt was weathered and frayed. The fabric had chosen exactly the wrong moment to break apart, as well.

Just as Marie, the girl he had longed to see for an entire year, had come drifting into view, the tie that held the sheath to his knife came loose, causing it to fall to the ground. Thoroughly embarrassed, young Simon got down from his horse and bent over to pick it up. As he stooped low, he noticed that Lucy and Kana Kó:re had stepped closer – and he could swear that he heard the maddening sound of girlish giggling.

Quickly, the young man made the repair to his belt, tying the sheath in place with a quick and simple not. Then, he hopped back up on his horse as several of the trappers accompanying his father's party approached Young John and offered their warm greetings.

Simon's face went red as he sat back in the saddle and glanced over at his lovely Marie. All winter long, Simon could not get her out of his mind. All winter long, he kept hoping for spring. All winter long, he begged his father to take him on the journey again this year – even though Emile seemed less than pleased with his son's complaining on the way home from the previous year's venture. But this was it. The time had come. He was only a few yards away from the girl that had bewitched his mind for the past six months.

Lucy and Kana Kó:re watched as the redness slowly flushed away from the young man's face. Lucy's heart skipped at the sight.

"He's no Ahentáken," Kana Kó:re said derisively.

Lucy kept silent. She wanted little more than to go over and speak to this handsome young man. And the last thing she needed was another argument with her pestering sister.

Just then, Simon swung his leg back over his horse and dropped back down to the ground. He straightened his shirt and dusted himself off a little before striding in the direction of the young Mohawk girls. All he could see as he approached was his Marie, though he could sense another set of eyes warm upon him.

Kana Kó:re donned a mischievous smile as the two girls stopped speaking and watched Simon come closer.

Kana Kó:re whispered something in Lucy's ear. Lucy chuckled.

Simon could feel his heart in his throat as he drew nearer. At that moment, the young man felt a strange sensation at his side – a sensation that was followed by a dull thud. He flailed wildly and then awkwardly looked at the ground. His knife had fallen again. He could feel his face flush with embarrassment a second time. With it, what little confidence he had dwindled almost entirely.

"Marie?" he said, his voice cracking as he bent down to pick up the errant knife again.

"Yes," Lucy responded with a slight giggle. "Would you like me to fix that?" She held out her hand to reach for the knife. As she did so, her fingers brushed against the knuckles of Simon's right hand.

The boy, startled by the sudden touch of Marie's rough fingertips, dropped the knife into the dust a third time. He sighed deeply, looking devastated.

Kana Kó:re laughed and walked back toward the house.

"No," Simon said, quickly picking the knife out of the dirt and dusting it off. "No, that's all right."

—⚜—

The Americans retreated southward through Montreal after their siege at Quebec was over. Will felt that this journey was a great deal different from his trek north only eight months prior. First of all – and most obviously – it was quite a bit warmer, this time around. Also, two thousand additional Colonial militias and regulars, who came bearing the gifts of food and fresh supplies, had recently reinforced his unit. And so, well fed and well supplied, the remnants of Arnold's troops began their march from Canada defeated, but with spirits raised.

With the eight thousand troops that the British had also sent to reinforce the location, the Colonials would not have stood a chance. The troop strength coupled with some deft and well-implemented British tactics simply made the already tenuous American position unsustainable.

Was it worth it? Will wondered. He had marched hundreds of miles to fight in a hopeless cause. *Maybe,* he thought. *With so many troops in Canada, there would be less in the colonies?* Certainly the long march home would give him plenty of time to reflect on the hardships he, his friends, and thousands of others had endured.

The journey would bring thoughts of Ben and David and how sorely he missed them. As the days grew longer and warmer and the seasons changed before his eyes, the young soldier marched on, surrounded by thousands of strangers and still feeling very much alone.

He recalled finding Ben's body. It had been among the hundreds of bodies that had drifted downriver with the spring thaw. Montgomery was there, along with dozens of troops who Will knew had been directly in his command.

The young man would never forget that bitter winter, everyone trying his best just to survive. Will saw himself as a changed man. He knew that to look upon the world as he did just over a year ago was not possible. With each footstep he took on the march southward, he could not get his friends, and his failure, out of his mind.

"Keep your eyes open!" came the command from down the line. "Mohawks have been known to side with the Lobsterbacks."

Will was lost in a memory of Ben. He had looked oddly peaceful when he had washed up on shore following the thaw. It brought comfort to the young man's heart, though not much.

"Hope we don't have to fight the Indians," a voice came from directly behind him in line.

Will turned and looked at the soldier marching behind him. "What?" he said in a bewildered tone.

"Indians!" the soldier said. "Ain't you been listenin'?"

"Listening to what?"

"Mohawks, cap'n says. They ally with the Brits."

Will looked the soldier over with a blank expression. All at once, he realized that he was a boy. His face was smooth and without stubble. His eyes were doe-like and innocent. If he had witnessed any death at the battle, he certainly did not show it.

He can't be more than fifteen, Will thought.

Just the same, the boy, wearing plain clothes and a large cocked hat, untied his musket along with all the other soldiers and continued the march with a charged musket and a watchful eye.

A crooked smile came to Will's face. It was strange, his new draw to conflict. *Mohawks don't love the Brits that much,* he thought. *At least not enough to attack an armed column of soldiers this size.*

Despite the promise of impending danger, Will's mind continued to drift and the march wore on. Once he arrived at the destination, he knew that he would be briefly discharged – and he also knew that he would use that brief discharge to visit the Bigelow farm in search of his Lucy. He hoped upon hope that Lucy would be home in the care of her mother and Jenny by the time of his arrival, but he knew in his heart that it was a fool's hope. Still, he settled on returning to the farm at the first opportunity.

As he resolved himself to this task, an old memory came floating into the forefront of his mind. In his mind's eye, he again saw young Lucy riding proudly out of camp.

She reined in her horse and looked down at him. "Good morning, Will. Have you come to see me off?"

Will had looked quickly at the ground. When he looked back up, he could hear himself saying, "Well...look, Lucy, I...I..." There are no words to express how awkward he felt at that moment.

"You take care of yourself, you understand?" he blurted. Then, more firmly (and, as he would later find out, prophetically), "And be on the lookout out for Lobsterbacks. They're out there, you know."

"I know," Lucy had said. "I'll be careful. And you take care, too, Will."

The young man's heart had fluttered at the words.

Lucy smiled, but it was a kind of smile that Will had not seen before. There was worry behind it – and in the brief time he had known this beautiful young woman, he had never seen her express anything but confidence.

Will nodded cautiously.

"I'm serious, Will!" she said in a chiding tone. "Do be careful. I...I want to be able to see you again when I come back."

Will nodded again, smiling this time. "I'll see you when you get back."

Will had waved, as Lucy turned southward with Private Weaver onto the main road.

And now, as he marched what felt like his hundredth mile of the day, Will's memory jumped ahead in time violently and without warning. He remembered one of the most devastating moments of his life. It was on par with the day David died. And the sight ranked alongside finding Ben dead in the river water.

It had been more than two years prior, now, but he remembered dismounting his horse and discovering the ghostly footprints by the oak tree. Even though he was not actually reliving the scene, he could still feel his heart nearly stop in agony.

"Lucy!" he had yelled. "Lucy!"

Ben and David had traveled with him that day and they followed Will in dismounting their horses. Will had pointed out the footprints – footprints that were clearly smaller and narrower than a man's – and then they split up and began searching the woods.

The young soldiers followed what appeared to be Lucy's tracks, which skirted around the darker edge of the trees and headed deeper into the woods. It did not take long before Will began to fear the worst. It appeared to his trained eye that Lucy had been trying to hide from someone or something.

Within a few minutes, Will had followed the tracks to the edge of a small clearing. The sun was shining brightly, and the flowers were thick and sweet smelling. But on the ground in front of him, his worst fears were realized. He could clearly see where those of at least three men had joined Lucy's footprints – and no matter how desperately he wanted to believe otherwise, Will Ashley was forced to admit that Lucy Killgrew had been taken prisoner.

His heart ached at the thought. Perhaps Lucy was indeed dead. Maybe the Brits had killed her.

At that moment, a second call rang down the line. And this time, Will heard it, because it was the worst kind of call: the call to arms.

If the retreating Colonials had assumed that they were being watched, they would have been correct. At a discrete distance, several men of all the clans in the surrounding landscape were posted along the route that had been leading the defeated army through their territory. For many miles, they had been scrutinized and analyzed and deemed to be less a threat than originally supposed.

Other eyes were watching, too. From the bottom of the ridge that the Colonials now crested, just at the edge of Young John's village, Kana Kó:re, Lucy, and several of the village's boys gazed up at the approaching army.

"How strange they all look together," Ahentáken said distantly.

Though she knew that these men could very well spell doom for both she and her new family, Lucy could not take her eyes off them. A more sensible young lady may have been compelled to run, but Lucy never was one to follow the rules – nor back down from a conflict.

"I don't think they look strange," Lucy said.

"That's because you look like them," Kana Kó:re said, laughing at her own observation.

Several of the boys laughed, too. All of them but Ahentáken, who kept his eyes transfixed on Lucy for a little longer than he should have.

Kana Kó:re seemed to notice, because she pushed Lucy softly in the back, nudging her in the direction of the ridge. *"Why don't you go talk to them?"* she asked with a smirk.

Lucy did not respond. *Maybe they want to harm me, as well,* she thought. She simply gazed up the grassy face of the hill hopefully, as though she may find a portion of her past if she just gathered the courage to run up to meet it. While she had to admit that the men did look a little odd in the clothes they were wearing, there was something vaguely familiar about them, too. She had seen this before. Still, nothing specific came to her mind – and it was agonizing.

Lucy's concentration was broken when she heard Kana Kó:re giggle. Lucy looked at her sister. *"What is it?"* she asked.

"Look there," Kana Kó:re said. *"Look at their hats!"*

She pointed up the hill, and the direction led Lucy's eyes to a young boy of maybe fifteen. His face was smooth and without stubble. His shoulders were stooped and scrawny. It was a boy and he was apparently a soldier. The hat on his head was indeed ridiculous – especially considering its contrast to his small body.

Lucy chuckled for a moment before noticing the young man walking next to this boy. The sight of him immediately caused her to stop laughing. She was struck with that same odd sense of familiarity. For some unknown reason, she wanted nothing more than to go to him. In fact, she did not just want to go to him, she wanted to run into his arms. It was peculiar; she had never felt anything like this before.

Kana Kó:re gave her sister another nudge, harder this time. *"Go on up there,"* she said. *"You know you want to."*

And Lucy's feet obeyed. One step followed another, and she found herself watching her feet rather than her destination; how could she be doing this? White men had driven her into the protection of Young John; white men had killed Kawehnákens. How could she know that these white men were safe?

Suddenly she heard a sound from above, and her head snapped up. The younger of the two soldiers was laughing. Laughing at her. He poked Will, breaking his concentration.

"Look," the younger one crowed. "I think the little Indian girls like us!"

"Are you crazy messin' with Mohawk girls?" Shouted Will.

Sorry, darlin'," the young soldier called down the hill. "His heart's sworn to a white girl!"

Lucy's tanned face turned beet red with shame, and she wheeled around and ran back to the others. By the time she reached them, she was sobbing.

"What did they say to you?" Ahentáken asked angrily.

Lucy trembled and shook her head. Kana Kó:re embraced her protectively.

"Let's just go," Kana Kó:re said. Lucy nodded, and the group of Mohawks retreated into the trees, the young soldier's laughter echoing in their ears.

Chapter Twenty-Two

Tekawí:iaks

Mohawk Valley, NY, August 1781

AS THE YEARS EBBED away, Lucy now thought of herself as Tekawí:iaks. With her lack of any real memory, she had become fully absorbed into the Mohawk society. Their joy was hers and their pain was hers.

These days, the only line to her former life – to her life as anything other than a proud young Mohawk maid – remained with Simon DuFore. Over time, she had become quite attracted to the young man. Each winter, she longed for his visits and, each autumn, she ached when he rode away.

Tekawí:iaks had blossomed into a beautiful young woman. Over the years, she had become fully fluent in the French and Mohawk language. English was but a distant and fading memory to her. In the summer, she looked very similar to all of her Mohawk counterparts – her hair dark and her skin bronzed from the many hours spent beneath the summer sun. Her true heritage only became apparent when winter came and her fair skin contrasted that of her sister.

Kana Kó:re had begun to treat Tekawí:iaks a bit more like a sister than she ever had before. The chief source of their disagreements, Ahentáken, had been joined to Kana Kó:re on the previous summer and, even before then, it had become clear to the Mohawk girl that her white sister was far more interested in the French boy who visited every spring, anyway. These days, the two were like the best of friends – and Tekawí:iaks could not help but think of Kawehnákens every time she shared a laugh with her now-beloved sister.

Even with the war in the colonies raging and the men of the village being called away, the Mohawk were blessed with four solid years of prosperous living, the villagers held many ceremonies giving thanks and showing respect to all that the land had to offer them. Tekawí:iaks would say a prayer of gratitude at the beginning of every day, as did all the villagers.

The sight to an outsider would have seemed rather marvelous. Against the backdrop of the rising sun, dozens of the villagers would emerge from their homes and bow in prayer, chanting beautiful and rhythmic incantations into the ground as well as the sky. Tekawí:iaks herself had struggled with her spirituality at first, but by now, it had become second nature. There was a peace in witnessing this kind of ceremonious sunrise, after all.

In the early spring, Tekawí:iaks would look forward to two things. The first, obviously, was the arrival of Simon, to whom she was growing closer with each passing year. And the second was banding together with the other villagers to gather maple syrup. Many parties of three or four would gather in the center of the village each morning and then head out into the woods to tap into the maple trees for their sweet syrup. It was quite a production.

Most mornings, Tekawí:iaks would say her prayer and then head to the center of the village, where Kana Kó:re and Ahentáken, who had built and moved into their own house since their marriage, would greet her. Tekawí:iaks had been left to live with her mother and father, the only remaining child in the home. It was a lonely feeling – particularly since, in spite of herself, she now longed deeply for a partner with whom she could share her life. But she had grown used to it. Young John did not seem willing to betroth her to any of the Mohawk boys. He never would have told his daughter, but he was secretly wondering if the whites would ever come to find her – and in that case, he did not want to make it any more difficult for her to be taken away than he already knew it would be.

So she would usually stroll up to the center of the village and wait for a matter of minutes for her sister and Ahentáken to arrive. On one particular morning, they had arrived rather late, both of them glowing in the early morning sunshine. The air was still chilly and there was still a few inches of snow on the ground.

"What took you so long?" Tekawí:iaks asked.

"Ahentáken, here, couldn't find his pick," Kana Kó:re said, ribbing her husband and smiling warmly as she looked into his eyes.

"What's so funny?" Tekawí:iaks asked.

Ahentáken laughed. *"It was under my pillow,"* he said.

"Yeah," Kana Kó:re added. *"He was sleeping on the pointy end of it all night and didn't even know where it was."*

Tekawí:iaks joined in the laughter.

"Anyway, are you ready?" Ahentáken asked, a soft light gleaming in his beautiful eyes.

Kana Kó:re and Tekawí:iaks agreed at once and the trio headed out into the woods.

The journey in past the tree line was often a long one because Ahentáken always swore that the best maples were deep within the forest. He always claimed to know of the most fruitful trees before he even set the spike into the bark, but both young ladies knew better. It was often three or four tries before their efforts bore any results. There were times, in fact, when they would drill into a tree only to realize that it had already been drilled on another side.

This particular morning was no different.

"This next tree, I know will spring syrup," Ahentáken boasted as the trio approached their fourth maple of the morning.

Ahentáken held his pick in his hand, which he swung back and forth by his side like a pendulum. Kana Kó:re held a sieve of deer intestine limply in her hand. Tekawí:iaks had been granted the difficult task for the day. She carried the large and heavy clay pot lined with wooden reeds. It was designed to hold the day's harvest of sap and, as a result, was terribly heavy. Tekawí:iaks knew that her task would only get worse once the pot was full, too. Ahentáken was likely to volunteer to carry it back for her, but in all the times he had suggested taking over, Tekawí:iaks had never relented. She could carry it on her own.

"That's what you said about the last one," Kana Kó:re said, smiling and winking at her sister.

"But this time, he means it," Tekawí:iaks offered.

Both girls laughed and Ahentáken turned around to glare at them – which, of course, only made them laugh harder.

"*I'll show you,*" he said, plunging his pick into the side of a solid and medium-sized maple.

After a few quick strokes, the tree did, indeed, begin to erupt slowly with sap.

"*See!*" the young man crowed.

Kana Kó:re chuckled and stuck the sieve into the hole her husband had created. Tekawí:iaks, in turn, aligned her clay pot beneath the other end of the sieve. Slowly but surely, the sweet treasure began to drizzle into the small hole at the top of the pot.

"*This one will fill us up,*" Ahentáken said. "*I can feel it.*"

"*Right,*" Tekawí:iaks said sarcastically. "*And I'll be the one who has to carry it.*"

As soon as the pot got too heavy, Tekawí:iaks set it down on the ground. Kana Kó:re, then, had to be more careful in guiding the still-sliding syrup into the small opening. Tekawí:iaks stared off through the trees, her eyes settling on a small patch of brush in a sunlit clearing as she thought about her Simon. He would be arriving any day now, she knew, and each day that passed brought more anxiety about his impending return.

Just then, she was snapped out of her reverie by a strange sensation on her shoulder. She turned at the sound of muffled laughter from her sister and Ahentáken. The sight of the both of them covering their mouths with the flat of their hands was funny on its own – right up until the moment Tekawí:iaks realized why they were laughing. A thick, sticky, cool sensation began slithering down her shoulder to her bare upper arm. Kana Kó:re was holding the sieve over her shoulder.

Tekawí:iaks jumped to her feet. "*What are you doing?*" she screamed, though she could not keep from smiling.

"Just thought you might like a shower," Kana Kó:re said, and her husband howled with laughter.

Tekawí:iaks laughed along, though she could not help but wonder how she was going to clean herself off before getting back to the village. The sun had warmed the air a little so she would not have to worry about the sap hardening in the time it took to walk back.

Still, she chuckled again. *"Fine, then. You're carrying this heavy thing back yourself. Serves you right!"*

Kana Kó:re doubled over. *"You know I can't lift that thing."* Then, she turned to her husband. *"Ahentáken, my dear husband...will you carry it for me?"*

Ahentáken agreed and the three of them headed back to the village with one full pot of syrup and one sticky arm between them.

In the summer, after the fields had been fully tilled, Tekawí:iaks would spend many hours planting with the women of all the clans. Each clan would help the others with planting in each individual field. The corn, beans, and squash would be planted together so that the beans would grow up clinging to the corn stalks and the squash would thrive in the shade of both.

One evening, after the day's planting had been finished, Kana Kó:re and Tekawí:iaks were walking back to the village when Ahentáken came riding up on his horse – a tall and muscular beast with a tan hide and a mane of dark black. Tekawí:iaks knew that Ahentáken was more proud of his horse than anything in the world except his beautiful wife, so she was always sure to tease him about it whenever she got the chance.

"That old mare of yours looks like it's going to break down any day now," she said amidst snickering from her sister.

Ahentáken, apparently having gotten used to the constant jabs, ignored her comment. *"Hello, my wife,"* he said. Then, donning a look of mock disgust, he added, *"And Tekawí:iaks."*

"Hello, my husband," Kana Kó:re said with a smile. *"You know, my sister and I were just discussing something that I think you would find interesting."*

"Really? What's that?"

Kana Kó:re smiled and elbowed her sister gently. *"Well, we spent all day planting the three sisters, and Tekawí:iaks pointed out that the three sisters reminded her of us."*

Ahentáken frowned thoughtfully. *"What do you mean?"*

"Well," Kana Kó:re continued, smiling broadly, *"Tekawí:iaks is tall and slender like corn. And I am short and small like a bean."*

"And what does that make me?" Ahentáken asked incredulously.

Tekawí:iaks laughed. *"A squash!"* she said.

Ahentáken climbed down from his horse and, in feigned anger, chased the young ladies all the way to the village.

During the snowy seasons, Tekawí:iaks would spend time listening to the elders and the stories they would tell. She would sit with Kana Kó:re during the day, making pelts, moccasins, and baskets – some of which would be traded with Tuck. The sisters made their own clothes from small bolts of cloth. She enjoyed playing "snow-snake," a game in which a pole would be tossed down a narrow trench carved in the snow. Everyone would taunt and yell at the thrower, hoping to break their concentration. Whoever threw the pole farthest would win. The sounds of laughter at this game would fill the village.

On the other side of the village, she and her sister

would watch the men working on strips of birch-bark and sticks, transforming the materials into strong canoes or heavy bows.

Even though a war had been raging for years all around the region, Tekawí:iaks felt safe and secure in the warmth and protection of the village. In fact, with each passing year, she became a little frightened by the thought of leaving it. Both she and Simon had spoken of it on many occasions, and while she had made plans with him to leave, she never realized that the day would be coming -- and coming soon.

Chapter Twenty-Three

The Last King

Hampshire, Massachusetts November 1781

NOTHING HAD CHANGED SINCE the last time Will had ridden up to the Bigelow farm. It was November of 1781 and there was a light dusting of snow on the ground. The land was peaceful and the earth slept lightly in preparation for the rebirth that would come in the spring.

"Why, Will Ashley," came the voice from inside the home as the front door swung open. "Thank God you're alive and well!"

Jenny Bigelow, wrapped tightly in a shawl, stepped out onto the porch.

"Yes, Miss Bigelow. It's sure surprised the heck out of me as well," Will replied, thinking of his experiences over the past few years.

"You've gotten old, son," Jenny said mournfully. "You all right?"

The young man straightened up in his saddle. He thought about swinging down to the ground, but then, for some reason, thought better of it. "Yes, I'm fine. Any word of Lucy?"

"Not a one," Jenny replied. "Wish I had. Lord, I miss that girl." As she spoke the words, she reflected on the young tomboy she once knew, riding hell-bent along the dirt road, the horse's hooves throwing up clumps of dirt as they flew by.

"Not a word, huh?" Will said, looking off at the horizon, which seemed to be dancing behind the lightly falling, windswept snow. "It's such a big country 'n all… and I'm thinkin' if she hasn't come home by now…" Intense frustration overcame him and he could not finish the thought.

"Her mother passed a few years back," Jenny said softly, pointing to the graves in the small, well-kept family plot next to the house.

Will looked to the little wooden markers and climbed down from his horse. He tied it to the porch and walked over to the graves. Peter, Jonathan, Tom, and Nancy lay neatly side-by-side, fenced in by a thorny, naked hedgerow.

"It looks a whole lot prettier in the spring," Jenny called from the porch.

Will remained silent, thinking of the many people lost during these terrible times. After a few moments of trying and succeeding in his battle against his own tears, he turned and walked back toward Jenny.

"Would you like to stay the night?" the tired-looking woman asked.

"No, thank you, ma'am," Will said. "I need to be gettin' on. We had a big victory in Yorktown, but there's more to do."

Jenny placed her hand on one of the splintery wooden posts on the porch. "Must ya go? You know you're welcome to stay here if you'd like."

"Why, thank you, Miss Bigelow, but no." Will reached into his coat and pulled out a letter, handing it to Jenny. "Would you please keep this?" he asked. "I wrote it for Lucy...for when she comes back. Maybe the Brits took her or she got hurt or -- "

"I'll put it in my keeping box," Jenny said, taking the letter from the young man's hand. "Just in case."

"Goodbye, Miss Bigelow," Will said. "I'm not sure if we'll see each other again, but I'll be thinkin' of you, anyhow." He then looked to the lonely grave markers and added, "And them."

"God bless you, Will Ashley," Jenny said, her eyes brimming with tears. "You take care of yourself, ya hear? And if you ever need a home, you come on back here."

"I thank you for that," Will replied. Then, he wheeled his horse around and rode off in the direction from which he'd come.

As Will slowly wandered atop his horse, he thought about the letter he had left for Jenny to give to his lost love. The memory of composing it was so vivid that he almost felt transferred back to the time and place when his pen first met the page. He could see himself sitting in the corner of the tavern, taking down his thoughts of the day. It had been a month earlier in Yorktown, shortly following the victorious battle that had been fought there on the part of the Colonials. The tavern was crowded and boomed in celebration as cups of ale clashed together with resounding words of cheers to "Washington, our boys, and the Frenchies!"

Do they know what we have done? Will remembered thinking. *Can they imagine the many sacrifices that were made to bring us to this day? Do they realize the lives lost?*

Will had grown quite bitter about the subject of war since seeing his best friends dead. No battle, however critical, however decisive, and however final seemed quite as sweet, these days.

And so, with the beer splashing and the drunken songs ringing all around him, the young man looked at all the smiling faces as the rowdy sounds began to soften and he penned the words:

> Dear Lucy,
>
> It has been so long since we last saw each other. For over four years, I did try you seek you out, but there were other obligations to attend to that for the very reason we celebrate today will attest.
>
> Oh Lucy, who would have dared imagine this day? The general of the British army, Lord Cornwallis himself, surrendering to us! I was told to arrange myself in line on one side of the road. Lucy, that line seemed to go on forever. I was within a hair's breadth of General Washington, who stood near the front. The French army was on the other side and their line stretched as far. Count Rochambeau led his men. Together, we marched toward the surrendering army.
>
> It seems now that George III will be our last king. We were all disappointed when Corn-

wallis did not make himself available. General O'Hara led the British through the line and then to a field, where they were to lay their arms on the ground. They seemed proud but defeated. They marched in a disorderly way. And when the order to ground arms was given, many threw their muskets down on the pile with tremendous force. Such a day.

Lucy, I am taking this letter to your mother in the hopes that it will find its way to you. This war will be over soon, or so I am told, and then we shall begin to build anew. It was my hope that, one day, we would be together, but it seems now that it will not be so. If I make it through this war, I will go back to Virginia and begin my life, but to do that, it is with a saddened heart that I must let you go and pray that you are well and content.

Yours,
Will

Will could remember studying that letter repeatedly in the days and weeks leading up to his arrival at the Bigelow farm. It had gotten to the point where he could recite it from memory. He regretted, now, mentioning of Lucy's mother in the letter; on the slim chance that the letter ever reached his love's hands; he did not want to upset her further. Still, he felt that the letter accomplished its purpose, explaining why he has ceased to look for her without sounding as if he no longer cared. Her soft hair and rosy skin, her sparkling brown eyes and sunny voice would always be a part of him.

As William Ashley pursued the horizon, he marveled at the surrounding countryside. Freshly removed from battle, it was as if he was looking at it for the first time. *Strange*, he thought, *I've never really noticed it before… this beauty…this life.* He pondered on how almost losing something makes a person appreciate it even more. It reminded him of the Killgrew family and how they were all gone now except for the little one. The idea of Jenny's pain and torment almost seemed to dwarf Will's own. She bore losing her son and husband. *Oh, the pain she must be holding inside.*

Then, unexpectedly, he smiled. He recalled Ben and David and how their shenanigans had so often brightened his day in even the worst of times. Their now-distant voices echoed in his head, softening the sounds of his horse's hoof beats upon the dirt road.

William Ashley survived the war and two terrible wounds. He returned home to Virginia and stayed near his sisters for a short time. One early morning he got up, and with only the clothes on his back and his trusty musket to his name, mounted his horse and rode off. No one ever heard from him again. Forlorn and without love or tribute, the young patriot vanished into history, leaving no trace except for a nation he helped create.

Chapter Twenty-Four

Reflection

Mohawk Valley, NY, September 1781

SIMON DUFORE HAD LEFT his father's hunting party early in order to return to the Mohawk village. The revolution ended a year ago and, feeling quite a bit safer, both he and his Marie, whom the Mohawks called Tekawí:iaks, had made plans to leave for Montreal and marry.

Each year that passed seemed to have been kinder to Tekawí:iaks than the last. She had grown into a beautiful young woman, and she wanted to go with Simon so badly that she could not stand it. Their yearly separation had begun to wear on the young woman, and she was eager to spend more time with her love. The only trouble was that she had also grown incredibly close to her surrogate family in that same span of time.

In the time it took for Lucy's identity to be lost and reshaped, Kana Kó:re and Ahentáken had fallen deeply in love, gotten married, and were now expecting their first baby.

Upon Simon's return to the village, he and Marie announced that the two of them would be leaving together to start a new life in Canada.

The news disheartened Young John. *"Daughter,"* he said, *"are you sure this man loves you?"*

"Yes," Tekawí:iaks said with a proud smile. *"I am sure."*

"And he will keep you safe?"

"Well ... no one will be as good at protecting me as you, Father," Tekawí:iaks said, embracing Young John firmly around his waist. He was still a head taller than she was, so she snuggled her cheek against his chest.

Young John smiled proudly. *"I have known Emile for many years,"* he said. *"He seems to have raised a good son."* Then, he donned a stern expression, which Tekawí:iaks had come to understand to mean that he was thinking deeply.

"He has, Father," Tekawí:iaks interjected.

"And he will provide for you?"

"Yes."

"Promise me one thing, Daughter," Young John said, grabbing Tekawí:iaks by the shoulders and putting a little distance between the two of them so he could look her in the eyes.

Tekawí:iaks nodded, tears forming in her eyes.

"Promise me that you will return one day. I do not want to part forever."

Whatever resolve the young lady had managed to maintain instantly evaporated. She began to sob like she never had before. Not even at the death of her little sister did she cry so openly. *"I will come every spring with Simon, if you desire it,"* she promised.

Young John remained silent. He knew that nothing would make him happier than to see his daughter every spring, but he understood that the trapping season was the most dangerous time of year. Therefore the forests and the streams in Spring would be no place for a lady. This he knew, yet he remained silent, hoping to see his daughter again. Tekawí:iaks understood her father's silence. She, too, knew that visiting him each year would be unlikely. In addition to the danger, she also that Simon, with all his protective love, enough to fill Young John's heart twice over, would never let her come.

At that moment, Kana Kó:re entered the stone house in which she and her sister had grown up. She saw that Tekawí:iaks was beginning to put her clothes and personal items into several bags. She, too, began to cry. *"Let me help you,"* she said. Then, she embraced her sister and cried even harder. *"I can't believe you're leaving. Please be safe."*

Tekawí:iaks suddenly had a vision of something long forgotten. The vision was of a woman. She looked nothing like Kana Kó:re, but Tekawí:iaks felt a strong affinity to her, nonetheless. She was older than her sister, but every bit as loving – and her gaze was about as kind and thoughtful as she had ever known. The eyes in this vision were also brimmed with tears, and as the woman opened her mouth to speak, the same words came out, though in a different language: "Please be safe."

Troubled, Tekawí:iaks snapped back to the present and returned her sister's embrace. She squeezed so hard that she was afraid Kana Kó:re might not be able to breathe.

Young John put a hand on the back of each of his daughters, rubbing them in a comforting fashion, clearly trying to avoid crying himself.

"*My daughters,*" he said. "*My beautiful daughters, how much joy you have brought into my life.*"

~§~

After she had finished packing her few possessions, Tekawí:iaks found herself back at the river – the one place she knew she could always come to when she needed to think. She sat on the riverbank as she had so many times, listening to the tranquil sounds of the water rushing by.

The only difference between this occasion and the many others was that Young John, eager to spend as much time with his departing daughter as he could, had come with her.

Tekawí:iaks looked at her father and said, "*I have never told you this, but when I look into the water and see my reflection, I let the river tell me my story.*"

Young John nodded proudly, though he was not sure what his daughter was trying to tell him.

"*You told me once that the river is very wise. Do you remember?*"

"*Yes,*" Young John said with a wistful smile. "*I remember.*"

Tekawí:iaks straightened up proudly. "*If you wait long enough, the river will show you many things. When I look into the river, I see my life here and all the happiness and sorrow. I see you.*" Then, with her eyes welling up with tears, "*I see Kawehnákens. Whenever I question my past, I let the river tell the story.*"

As Young John crossed his hands in front of his chest, Tekawí:iaks gazed back into the water. All at once, the past rushed over her like a flood.

She saw herself lying in a canoe full of animal pelts as

her slightly younger father stood on the opposite end and paddled downriver. To her, this was the first moment of life. All else before it, even when she was gazing into the river, was impossibly hazy and distant.

What came next in the line of visions was troubling. It was her deliverance. She saw herself rising to her feet, musket in hand, dispatching a vicious Huron as he charged upon her father. At that moment, she knew she was inextricably linked to the man who had offered her passage down the river and safe shelter from the wilderness. Before she even knew what Iroquois meant, she now understood that, regardless of her past, it was part of who she was.

The point was reinforced as Tekawí:iaks had a vision of her first day in the village. Konwáhne, her new mother, reached out to her with a hesitant hand and a kindly set of eyes. Kawehnákens, poor Kawehnákens, was quick to latch on to her leg – a position that Tekawí:iaks grew quite used to over the fleeting year that followed. Then she saw Kana Kó:re. She returned Tekawí:iaks' gaze with an icy stare – another common theme for the coming months.

Then suddenly, a rapid succession of visions flooded Tekawí:iaks' memory from the surface of the river. She reflected on Kawehnákens in the cornfield, running with two corncobs on her head, charging after her like a bull. She witnessed the tracking game, in all its repeated glory, as though she had played it only yesterday. Then, inevitable when she thought on Kawehnákens, she saw Young John carrying her limp body back to the village. Finally, she witnessed again that terrible, sad day of mourning as they placed her small body in the shallow grave.

A crippling notion then struck Tekawí:iaks. *What a beautiful young girl she would have been*, she thought.

Again, the memories lapped over her like waves. She recalled evenings around the fire, with the family gathered to teach Tekawí:iaks a new word in Mohawk. The concept of having to learn Mohawk seemed strange, at this point. Now, she had such a command of the language that she could hardly recall English anymore. However, back then, as she learned, she would stare transfixed at the glowing coals warming and lighting up the smiling faces whenever she got a word wrong.

She remembered Young John's many departures with the other men during the war. Mostly, they had been scouting missions, or so Young John told her. In reality, the Mohawk and other nations that allied themselves with the British had raided colonial settlements in New York and Pennsylvania.

The was and the missions meant little to until one day in 1779 she began to see many new faces from different tribes passing through her village. All had escaped massive colonial raids on villages throughout New York. Survivors had flowed in with only the clothes on their backs and a few meager possessions. Stories of the raiders burning homes, and destroying crops and fields were common. Some stayed, but most would left as soon as it was safe for them to do so. Young John had told her that one day soon they too might have to uproot their village and head north to Canada to be under the protection of the British. However, for now, the colonial army had stopped short of her village and returned to Tioga. She felt some comfort in that.

She remembered Kana Kó:re as a girl of sixteen: it was hard now for Tekawí:iaks to believe that they could have been so distant during the early years. Her smile was the most warming thing she had ever witnessed. They were indeed and always would be sisters, if not by blood, then by heart.

As the visions ebbed, Tekawí:iaks realized that she was

simply sitting on the edge of the riverbank as she had done so many times before. She was aware of her father's presence, but did not acknowledge it right away. For the time, she reflected on the many occasions she had come to the riverbank and sat on the same old log on which she now sat, watching the flow as it moved swiftly past the larger stones.

At that moment, she had an idea – and it struck her like a thunderclap, urging her to move forward. She stood carefully, kicked off her moccasins, and waded into the crystalline water, still chilly from the mountain runoff.

"Daughter, what are you doing?" Young John asked, standing and reaching out his hand in protest.

Tekawí:iaks did not speak a reply. She just nodded her head reassuringly and smiled, holding her hand out to signal that her father should remain on the shore.

"The water is very cold," Young John said desperately.

However, Tekawí:iaks did not hear. She picked up a small blue-green stone and waded deep in the frigid water. Slowly, she had bent forward, allowing her long, beaded hair to float. All she could hear now were the liquid sounds of the riverbed and her father's muffled cries.

"Tekawí:iaks," Young John barked, *"you'll drown."*

At that moment, Tekawí:iaks stuck her head out of the water, smiled, and said, *"I'm okay, Father. Let me be. I may never get the chance to speak with the river again."*

Concerned as he was, Young John did as he was asked. As he wandered back to the village, he began to realize that his new daughter's spirituality was very strong. He knew as she did that it was a living, breathing presence. That which was locked within her for so long was trying to come to the surface.

With her head back in the river, Tekawí:iaks basked

in the rejuvenating silence and peace. Truly, this lapping current held all the answers for which she had ever searched. Within minutes, many trout gathered in curious wonderment of this strange apparition. They darted all around her, sometimes brushing up against Tekawí:iaks' legs, sometimes nibbling at her hair.

Tekawí:iaks laughed inwardly at the feeling, wondering how such life could have eluded her for so long. She felt entirely removed from herself. She was one with the river and all the spirits within.

Suddenly, something stripped away her environment and left her standing in blackness. Where once there was the gaggling sound of the current, there was now only silence. Where once there was trout, there was only a distant breeze. All sense of sight and comprehension drained out of the young girl, and she felt both relieved and terrified at once.

"Hello?" she said, in a language that she had long since ceased to speak. "Where am I?"

"*Who* are you?" *asked* a motherly voice from out of the blackness. The voice was familiar and yet unfamiliar.

"I am ... I am ..." Tekawí:iaks said, unable to find the answer. She was terrified. For a moment, she saw herself lying in Young John's canoe atop the animal pelts once again. She could not explain who she was or from where she had come.

"Lucy," the voice said. It was kinder now, gentler. "Is that you, Lucy?" Tekawí:iaks' heart leapt into her throat. She felt as though she had just discovered a long-forgotten treasure that she had buried long ago. *Lucy*, she thought. *Who is Lucy?*

All at once, she recalled a small connection that she had lost – a longing that she had carried for years and could not quench. It was as though she had been walking around empty for longer than she could remember, yet she had just realized that the hole had never been filled. Instead, she had simply begun to ignore it, as if the hole had never existed in the first place.

"You are Lucy," the voice repeated. "Never forget that."

"*I do not understand,*" Tekawí:iaks said in Mohawk. She wanted nothing more than for that to be the truth. She needed to know her past, her identity, but every ounce of her wanted to give up the search, ignore all that had come before her passage down the river with Young John. Yet, the name Lucy -- it bore meaning. The water turned to a vision of a window. She was looking through it into the black, cold night. She heard herself say, "Why hasn't Father come yet, Mother? He said he would be here for my birthday, and today *is* my birthday. Oh, Mother, he must come. He simply must!"

She heard the motherly voice coming from behind. "Lucy, you've been sitting on that settle and asking me that same question all day. Your father will be here if he can, you know that. However, don't get your hopes up. Your father has much weighing on his mind."

It pained her to hear it, but she knew she must always keep what she heard safe and close to her.

She accepted the name in that instant, but gave it no more or less significance than Tekawí:iaks or Marie. Still, she could not help but acknowledge the weight it seemed to place on her heart.

Lucy, she thought. *I am Lucy.*

Suddenly, the blackness faded away, parting like the dark hair unfurling before her eyes as it danced in the streaming water. She opened her hand and there in her palm was the blue-green stone. She looked down and saw more stones, hundreds of them shaped and polished by this same river for thousands of years. She upended her hand and the stone fell purposefully to the bottom, blending in with the others. She lifted herself out of the water and said, *"I will leave now and my story will rest in the river."*

Contented, she walked back to the village to join with Simon and to say her long goodbyes to the family of villagers who cared and nurtured her over the years.

"My story will rest in the river."
— Tekawí:iaks

Chapter Twenty-Five

Stephanie

Montreal, Canada, Present Day

CELESTE SAT, MESMERIZED BY the story that her grandfather had just related. She looked at the portrait again, its eyes seeming to have shifted as though deep in thought, and asked, "But what happened to her, Grandfather? What happened to Marie?"

"Well," the old man said. "She settled in and raised her family." He stood up slowly, pushing heavily with his weakened hands against the armrests of his comfortable antique chair. He paused for a moment then turned to his granddaughter with a puzzled look on his face.

"You know," he said. "Marie's first born, Thomas, said that just before Marie passed away at an old age, she began to speak in English and mentioned something about her father teaching her to fire a musket. Of course old people say funny things sometimes. But Thomas hadn't known his mother even spoke English."

"But that means she remembered," Celeste said happily.

"Eventually, yes, it seems she did," Grandpa Henri said. He thought on what he had just said. "But if you're interested in knowing more about Marie, everything you want to know is right here in this house. Right here in these books for you to read." He gestured to his expansive bookshelves.

"There's more information about Marie in these books?" Celeste asked, barely able to contain her excitement.

"Yes, little one, right here."

Celeste stood up and walked over to stand beside her grandfather. She gazed at the spines of the dusty and weathered books, all of them a deep hue of red, brown, or purple. "Like what?" she asked, not taking her eyes off the books.

"Well, for one thing...Marie kept a diary. Apparently, she was very fond of writing down everything that happened in her family." Henri DuFore grabbed a book off the shelf, looked it over for a moment, and then shook his head. Then, he hobbled out of the study and down the hallway a few paces, turning into his library. Inside, the shelves of old and very old books stacked row after row, from floor to ceiling, traversing each wall completely.

"In here," the old man called as soon as he realized his granddaughter had not followed.

In a moment, Celeste wandered in, her eyes wide as she held a book in her hand and gazed around the room. She had been in this room only once before, but as a young girl, it had never carried much interest for her. Until this point, it had just seemed old and musty. The smell of old paper permeated the room.

"Wow," she breathed.

"Sit down, little one," Grandpa Henri said.

Celeste followed his command without hesitation, positioning herself in an old leather armchair and watching as her grandfather shuffled over to the shelf of books on the far wall. For the first time, Celeste noticed that a glass panel protected one of the sections – the one furthest to the left and standing at about eye-level to her grandfather. The panel appeared to have hinges, and obviously operated like a door.

Celeste watched with baited breath as Grandpa Henri opened a drawer in an old wooden desk near the panel and pulled out a small ring of keys. The keys were all long and skeletal, just like the ones she had seen in mystery movies. The old man carefully selected a key and inserted it into the locked glass door. He carefully swung the panel open and stuck his hand inside. In a moment, he pulled out a leather-bound book, easily the oldest and most delicate that Celeste had ever seen. Without even asking, she knew it was the diary that her grandfather had spoken of.

Grandpa Henri smiled as he turned to face his granddaughter. He had read the diary he now held many times and was quite familiar with the young adult life of Marie DuFore.

"I've always found that it was Marie's early life that was most interesting," he said, handing the diary over to Celeste. He watched as his granddaughter, her mouth hanging open in awe, carefully separated the cover from the first page.

"Now…" he continued with a tone of caution. "When you want to read it, the key will be in this drawer." He pointed to the drawer from which he had first retrieved the key. "But listen to me, my child," he said.

Celeste turned her head away from the book and looked squarely at her grandfather.

"You must never leave this house with this book," he said. "Do you understand me?"

"Yes," Celeste said, meaning it with every ounce of her energy.

"It is very valuable, you see? One day, it will be in your care...but in the meantime, it will be in this case whenever you want it."

"I will be careful," Celeste replied sincerely.

Grandpa Henri smiled widely. He had always been proud of his Celeste, but words simply could not describe the level of pride that he now felt. His granddaughter was truly interested in the history of her family – and it had happened to her right around the same time it had happened to him. He recalled the day that he had first encountered Marie's journal as if it had happened yesterday.

"And now," the old man said, "I need to get some rest. I'll get out of your way and let you read. But don't let me rest too long."

"I'll wake you in an hour or two," Celeste said, not looking up from the pages of the journal.

To my journal
June 7, 1785

Today I was determined to speak with Simon about going to the village.

I miss my family and would like to be with them before the baby arrives.

Simon is very stubborn about letting me go but I think I am getting him closer to saying yes. I will go to the chandlery where I hope.....

Rue St Pierre, Port of Montreal 1785

Marie DuFore drew her shawl closer to her neck to warm her from the cool wind blowing from the St Lawrence. She walked briskly past the old seminary and continued toward Chandlery De Bateau De DuFore (DuFore's Ship Chandlery). Simon had completely surprised everyone by having a remarkably good head for business. Simon sold many of the items he and his father trapped, hunted or traded to sailors newly arrived at the port. It soon got to a point where these items were not enough, and soon he and Marie opened their warehouse. Over the next few years the business grew and expanded from trading pelts and other local items to food and other provisions that the departing ships would need to feed their crews. While it was a little overwhelming at first, she soon got used to the daily comings and goings of seamen and ships

At various intersections she would pass small groups of British soldiers and remembered how on the day she arrived became nervous at the sight of the men in the red coats. She would pass them by and they would stare at her and she in turn would briefly look in their direction so as not to appear to be avoiding their glances. After all she was French and they were English and there still was a little mistrust between the two societies. However, with the passage of time and the peace and order that they brought with them, she soon came to accept their presence without concern.

She remembered how crowded Montreal seemed to her on her first day out of the wilderness. Horses and carriages clattering over the cobble stoned streets, the din of the merchants shouting over one another, holding up their wears. The smell of fish permeated the sir and in the heat of summer sun, sometime the stench was unbearable. The beautiful clothes the people wore in a multitude of colors were like moving rainbows to her.

Evenings were exciting and alive within the city's core. Quite a difference from the calm and serene nights she experienced in the Mohawk village. The peace she sought within herself gazing up at the stars was gone forever. How she missed her Mohawk family. At given moment of the day she would find herself wondering that they were doing. She could see them as clear as if they stood beside her. They were beneath the same sky, the same moon and the same sun. *Were they thinking of me?* she would think.

Marie was pregnant and before she was too far along she wanted to visit the village, but convincing Simon had proved daunting. He was very protective of his wife and unborn child, and he felt the journey would prove too stressful for her. Marie would not give up until she had exacted every trick she knew.

Toward the end of April, Marie had given a hunting party a message to be delivered to Young John in the land of the Mohawk. Her message asked her father to come up with a way to convince Simon and her father-in-law Emile to let her come to them. Since then two hunting parties had been turned back and denied access to Mohawk land. Both had returned to Montreal saying Simon DuFore of Montreal would explain the reason for denial.

Simon was with one of the trappers when Marie entered the store. They were not happy and now Simon would have to give in to Marie and let her go. He truly loved her and had decided earlier to allow the journey to the village.

"Ah my wife enters," he said pretending surprise and wonder. "Jean, have you met my wife Marie?" he said to the trapper. "She is now the one that controls commerce."

"What are you talking about?" she asked.

Simon explained what had happened to the trappers on Mohawk land and as he continued the explanation, she thought about Young John. *He must want me to come as much as I want to go,* she thought. *I never thought he would go this far.*

"Simon," she said, surprised. "I thought he would send you a gift. I never thought that he would do this."

"So," he said with a loving smile. "You had better go then. Leave tomorrow." He paused for a moment and then said, "I'll get some of my men to go with you."

Marie gave Simon a hug. "Thank you, my husband," she said and hurried toward the door before he changed his mind.

"And Marie..."he said

She turned to face Simon.

"Don't forget to take Jean and his men. They have families to feed. Speak to the Mohawk."

"Certainly," she replied coquettishly.

More than an hour later, Celeste looked up from her reading and glanced at the ornate, antique clock resting above the desk. The phone was ringing and she was startled to realize how much time had passed. Truly, she had been lost in a book for the first time in her life. The room was alive with history.

The telephone continued to ring. Normally, Celeste would be home from church by this time and her mother would be checking her daughter's whereabouts. *It's mother,* she thought. *I'll let grandpa take the call. It will wake him up.*

I better put this book away for now, she thought. *I can't wait to read more tomorrow.*

She walked over to her grandfather's special glass enclosure and opened it carefully. However, as she gazed inside, she could not help but be curious about some of the many other books resting inside. There are so many, she thought, all leather-bound, just like Marie's journal! She pulled several out and looked at them. One had the same elegant, slanted handwriting as the book she had just read; this one was obviously written by Marie as well. Another was written in heavy, masculine slashes. Oh, why had she told her grandfather she'd be done in a couple of hours?

As if on cue, Grandpa Henri stood in the entrance to the study, a broad smile on his face. "I just got an interesting phone call from someone named Stephanie McAllister. I told her that I thought you should talk to her."

"What did she want?"

Her grandfather handed her a slip of paper with an American telephone number on it. "Why don't you call her and find out?"

Chapter Twenty-Six

Jackson

Hampshire, Massachusetts, Present day

OLD MAN JACKSON SAT alone on his porch watching the sun dance near the horizon. Grabbing hold of the loose ends of the blanket he wore over his shoulder, he wrapped it snuggly around his neck as the sun disappeared behind a billowing stream of white clouds, taking with it the warmth and exposing the old man to the cold.

Although the old house remained relatively unchanged over the many years, Jackson's farm had ceased to be a farm a long time ago. Instead of a farm, the trees and the land were just considered acreage. Mother Nature had reclaimed the once fertile fields with young pines and tamaracks.

Beneath the trees, flowering bushes bloomed in the spring with berries and an abundance of wild flowers. The colors and smells of the land attracted many birds – bobolinks, meadowlarks, finches, sparrows and hummingbirds.

With the approach of winter, Jackson knew that the deer, moose, and other animals would winter here, feeding on the remaining morsels of plant life and seeking out old man Jackson's forest for protection. During the school year, children would come in buses to study the boundless forms of wildlife during the changing seasons.

Since today was Thanksgiving Day, the old man wondered if anyone would show up to visit with him.

Jackson was the last of his line. His wife had passed away three years ago, and his son had been taken in Vietnam. Now, all that he had left was his old house, his beautiful land, and the sound of the breeze rustling through the large tamaracks close by.

Still, despite all the melodrama in his mind, old man Jackson knew that a visitor would arrive eventually. Taking an odd and palpable pity on his lonely state, the townspeople always elected someone to stop by with some holiday cheer. Yet, every year that came, he could not help but wonder if that would be the year that he would finally be forgotten.

However, this day was different. This day, he was not waiting for a town-appointed guest. This day, he had invited guests of his own – and he could not have been more excited about their impending arrival.

He watched eagerly as the car he saw in the distance pulled onto the road that would bring it to his farmhouse. His steely blue eyes worked hard to focus on the approaching car. As it got closer, his heart sank. He recognized the car, and knew instantly that it was not carrying the people he had hoped. "Happy Thanksgiving, Jack old man," Fred said as he stepped to the side and opened the back door of the car, stooping over to pick something up from within.

"Happy Thanksgiving, Jack!" Alice beamed.

"Happy Thanksgiving," Jackson responded blandly. "You lose the toss?"

Alice frowned.

"I keep telling them I'm all right," Jackson continued, staring off into the distance.

"Oh, come on now," Alice said. "Don't be like that. It's time to celebrate! You should be more cheerful."

Old Jackson knew more than anyone did what this holiday was about, but he just nodded his head and politely smiled, acknowledging the effort by this couple to be kind and neighborly.

"Martha at the post office told us you'd be having company today, so we won't tarry," Alice said.

"Yessiree," Fred continued, "just wanted to stop by and bring you some turkey and our best wishes for the holiday."

For the first time, Jackson noticed what Fred was carrying. He held what looked like a full turkey in a giant plastic container. As delicious as he knew the turkey would be, the old man could not seem to sway his thoughts from the visitors he was truly anxious to see. As such, he kept one eye on his company and one eye on the road in the distance. "I thank you for that," he said.

Alice looked around at the well-maintained buildings and land that Jackson had managed to keep. "You sure have a wonderful piece of property, Jackson," she said awkwardly. "So magnificent!"

"Yessir, it's one of a kind," Fred said. Then, he added softly, "Too bad the town's gonna get it all."

Fred's words cut right through Jackson. At that moment, he had visions of his son. He remembered his boy heading off to war with a heavy heart and a head hung low. Painfully, he remembered receiving the letter informing him of his son's death. He had hoped to pass the farm on to his son. Since that was now impossible, at least he was assured that the farm would be preserved forever under the protection of the town, as would the family name of Bigelow.

In September of that same year, Stephanie McAllister, through the process of researching Lucy Killgrew, found a reference to the DuFore family. Since Celeste had returned Stephanie's call to her grandfather a few months ago, she and Stephanie have communicated and researched their shared past.

Before long, Stephanie had received a call from Jackson Williams, a direct descendant of Jenny Bigelow Pratt. Jackson invited both of the young ladies to the farm over the Thanksgiving holiday. He told them that they could see the land where so many of their ancestors had lived and could ask him whatever questions they wanted.

Even though Jackson had forgotten more than these girls already seemed to know, the call had piqued his interest greatly – and it was truly the first thing in which he had taken any kind of interest in years.

The old man, annoyed by the presence of the Turners, continued to scan the distant road for signs of another vehicle.

"Sure you'll be okay, Jack?" Alice asked with clear concern as her husband placed the plastic container of turkey on the porch by his feet.

"Don't worry about me," Jackson replied. "I'm used to being on my own. In fact, I prefer it these days. Gives me a chance to think."

"Well, all right, then, Jackson," Fred said. "It was real nice seeing you. Hope you have a wonderful holiday."

Jackson cringed. He appreciated the effort – but really,

charity had never been something that he thought he needed. He may have been lonely, but he was not dying; and whenever he received one of these visits, that is exactly how he felt.

Just as Fred and Alice began to climb back into their car, Jackson's heart skipped. In the distance, along the horizon, a minivan slowed down and made the turn onto his road.

With a wave and a smile, Fred and Alice drove off, heading in the direction of the approaching van. As soon as the two automobiles met up, they stopped, and Jackson could see that Fred had rolled down his window and was conferring with the driver of the minivan. In a moment, Fred pointed in the direction of Jackson's house.

Shortly after Fred waved, the cars parted, and Fred and Alice took off in one direction while the van headed up the hill toward Jackson.

Jackson stood up from his chair as the van came to a stop in his driveway. The doors swung open and out stepped two girls of about fourteen. Though the old man had never met them, he knew immediately that they were Celestine DuFore and Stephanie McAllister. An older woman and man accompanied them.

The girls skipped up and introduced themselves. "Are you Jackson Williams?" Stephanie asked with a smile.

"Yes, I'm Jackson," Jackson said, excited to have invited company for the first time since he could remember. "But you can call me Jack, if you like."

The elderly woman was the next to approach after the girls. She seemed very sprite and nimble for her age. "Hello," she said, extending her hand for Jackson to shake. "I'm Betty McAllister. Stephanie's grandmother." She smiled warmly at her granddaughter. "And this gentleman is Henri DuFore. Celestine's grandfather."

Henri struggled to climb the steps up to the covered

porch. He steadied himself on the wooden railing that stretched around the porch and trailed down the steps.

"They've been planning this little trip for months," said Betty with a bright, proud smile. "Bless their hearts."

Old Jackson returned the smile – which felt strange to him since he had not really smiled at anyone in months. "Well, c'mon in then," he said. "I guess I shouldn't keep them waiting any longer."

"Yes," Henri said. "Such inquisitive minds." Henri and Celeste spoke fluent English with only a slight hint of a French accent.

Jackson laughed and swung his front door open. The girls were the first to charge inside. The two of them walked from room to room, studying everything with clear excitement.

"So this is it?" Stephanie asked, looking wide-eyed around the small living room.

"This is it," Jackson replied. "Hasn't changed since it was built in 1755 by my ancestors, Peter and Jenny Bigelow." He led everyone to the kitchen and sat down. "Have a seat," he said.

"Now, take your time and look around." He watched as the two girls slowly glanced around the room. "The kitchen was the pivotal point of the house. Everything happened in this room."

Stephanie and Celeste could both feel Lucy's presence in the room. On her last night in the house, Lucy made her way to the kitchen quietly after she was sure everyone was asleep, looking for a little food to sustain her on her journey.

Then, Jackson looked conspiratorially at the girls and added, "I suppose you want to see it..."

"Yes please," Celeste replied eagerly, clapping her hands together.

"In a minute," the old man said. "Let's go back on the porch and sit a while. I want to tell you a few things."

"I think that is a good idea," Henri said with a sigh. "These old bones are tired."

Jackson looked at him and smiled. "I have another blanket in the linen closet, if you'd like." Without waiting for a reply, Jackson went into the closet and retrieved the blanket.

When everyone was seated in rocking chairs on the side of the porch that faced the tree-lined back yard, old man Jackson pointed to the left. Surrounded by a small hedge, a clearing appeared. For centuries, four tall tamaracks have guarded this special place. "It's over there," he said. "The Bigelows and the Killgrews were the best of friends, you see. In fact, I heard many stories about their friendship while I was growing up. Sometimes, if I listen very closely at night…you know, when everything gets quiet … I can hear the voices of all the generations mixed together. Most of the voices telling the story of Lucy Killgrew." He touched Celeste's nose and said, "The one from which you are directly descended."

Celeste gushed with pride.

"And you know, I saw you on the news, Stephanie. I'm not sure if I told you this, but when I heard you mention Lucy Killgrew on a news program, that's when I decided to call you."

They spoke about the past for an hour or so before Stephanie said, "I am a descendant of Daniel … Lucy's brother. What happened to him?"

Jackson sighed, leaned back in his rocking chair, and looked up at the sky for a moment as he collected the memory. "Nancy died in childbirth and gave Daniel over to Jenny to raise as her own. Jenny remarried a man named Samuel Pratt and Daniel was raised as theirs. She waited until he was old enough before telling him about his real parents.

Daniel Killgrew eventually became a captain in the Continental Army after serving honorably at Fort McHenry in Baltimore, Maryland during the War of 1812. That's when Francis Scott Key wrote the Star-Spangled Banner."

He paused briefly, and then continued. "Jenny had two children with Pratt. I'm all that's left of their line."

"May we see it now?" Celeste asked eagerly.

Jackson nodded and rose from his chair. When the group had managed to descend the few stairs, Jackson took both girls by the hand, Stephanie on the left and Celeste on the right. Henri and Betty walked behind, grinning from ear to ear as they watched their granddaughters. They moved across the compound toward the four large trees that stood guard over the small clearing. There, just below their feet, Jenny and Peter Bigelow, and Nancy and Tom Killgrew rested in eternal peace. The grounds were well kept and, the original wooden markers had been replaced with stone.

Jackson looked up at the tall tamaracks, their bare branches grabbing hold of the sky and said, "Jenny insisted on being buried here. Supposedly, her last request was to be the fourth tree; trees that she and Nancy planted. Pratt and the others are in the county cemetery just outside of town."

The air was strangely still, except for a slight wind howling through the rafters of the nearby stable. There they were: Stephanie stood on the same spot where once a young William Ashley stood so long ago, perhaps silently saying goodbye in much the same fashion that she was now saying goodbye.

Was it something beyond the reach of this mortal world that had enticed a recluse like old man Jackson to invite the relatives of his family's distant friends to spend the night? He had quickly developed a fondness for the wide-eyed inquisitiveness of the two girls. He treasured his family history and respected the past, a past shared by the four people now sleeping under his roof.

Given the knowledge of what happened In Nancy Killgrew's room so long ago, the old man had offered the girls another room to sleep. They were undeterred.

The two cousins did not know that they would share more than a bed that night. In the same room that was Nancy Killgrew's up to the time of her passing, they were about to share a deep spiritual connection.

Around eleven o'clock in the evening, Celeste threw down the heavy comforter from around her neck and fluffed it under her arms. The cold, blowing wind outside pushed against the side of the old house. Its timbers and planks protested with groans, creaks and yawns. Naked branches like huge fingers scratched and tapped against its wooden sides and windowpanes.

"The house is speaking," whispered Stephanie.

Celeste had not realized that her cousin was also awake and felt somewhat relieved. She turned to Stephanie and asked, "Are you scared?"

"No," she quickly replied.

"Me neither," said Celeste. "No harm can come to us under this roof."

"I know," replied Stephanie. "I think everything about us being here is good."

Suddenly, they detected another sound. This sound was much different caused by the wind and it was coming from just outside their room.

"What's that?" asked Celeste.

"Go look," Stephanie replied.

"Together?" asked Celeste.

"Together," responded her cousin.

The two girls climbed out of the bed and walked cautiously to the door.

With their ears pressed against the door, they heard footsteps walk past and move down the stairs.

They knew the main door had opened below because cold, night air rushed up the stairs and pushed against their bedroom door.

"Maybe it's Mister Jackson," said Celeste with a look of uncertainty.

Stephanie, recalling her past experience with Lucy, whispered, "Maybe not."

Celeste looked at her, "You think it's .... "

As the words left her mouth, the front door slammed shut. Instantly, everything fell silent. The wind stopped blowing and the noises ceased. The house seemed to exhale.

The girls quickly tip toed to the window and looked down in the yard below. They could see the family plot and the four trees standing watch. Then they noticed movement in the corner of their eyes. A tear rolled down Stephanie's cheek when she recognized the form below.

"Is it...?"

Stephanie nodded.

A soft rap sounded on their door and in walked Betty, Henri, and Jackson. They, too, had heard the commotion but thought it was the girls.

Celeste turned and motioned for them to come closer. They huddled together and watched through a spiritual glow as the colonial tomboy, her musket slung over her shoulder, disappeared through the large barn door. They could hear the horse blowing impatiently and the sound of its hoofs pounding the ground in anticipation of the rider.

"Oh my," said Henri holding his hand to his mouth.

"Is that Lucy?" asked her grandmother.

With her eyes glued to the window, Stephanie nodded.

"There are no animals in there," said Jackson. "Not for years."

Lucy Killgrew reappeared through the barn doors leading her ghostly stallion into the yard. Just as she did over two hundred years ago, she looked up at her mother's window, and then mounted her horse.

Holding the animal steady with one hand and waving a silent goodbye with the other, she pulled the reins to the right and rode away.

Without saying another word, the family retired to reflect on what they had the privilege to witness.

Early the next morning standing once again by the grave markers, the girls thought back to the night before.

Turning to her cousin, Celeste asked, "Do you think she will be back?"

"I think she will always be with us, because she's a part of us," replied Stephanie.

Then looking at the markers once again, Celeste added, "They all are."

There was one question still remaining on Stephanie's mind. She turned to Celeste and asked, "Why do you think Lucy came to me? Why not you?"

"My grandfather is very wise," Celeste replied. "He once told me that every family has ghosts, and it is our lack of knowledge about who they were that stills their souls, but sometimes makes them restless. I think Lucy knew that you were going to Mayfair and that you could help her find the muskets. I think she knew you were ready to receive her wonderful gift."

The two girls could not imagine that far away to the west in the Mohawk Valley near Canajoharie, a river twisted and flowed past the site of what once was a Mohawk village. The old log on which the young colonial tomboy named Tekawí:iaks sat so long ago searching for her identity, had crumbled into a brown dust. As with everything in life, Nature had reclaimed what was hers. The forests and fields were now a hiker's paradise. Anyone stopping at the river-bank to rest and cool themselves might take notice of a beautiful blue-green stone lying in the shallows.

While Celeste and Stephanie removed the dried leaves around the cold stone markers, they spoke of the hard-ships and the sacrifices their ancestors made so long ago. They promised each other to keep their loved ones alive by sharing their stories with each succeeding generation. The ground upon which they all stood was sacred. It was the place where two families answered the call for their country and offered up all that they had for each other. At this place, an ancient family bond, once lost, was rediscovered: Two cousins separated by time, a national border, and a language, finally came together at a small Massachusetts farm.

The End